JANE DOE CATHERINE 3

BY KRIS CALVERT

Cover by jim@insigniadesign.com
Edited by Meg Weglarz and Molly J. Kimbrell

ISBN: 978-1-943180-25-7

Calvert Communications, Lexington, KY 40515

Acknowledgements

Thank you to **Jim**, my friend and colleague for over twenty-five years. You are by far the best designer in the world. I'm so privileged to know you and am thankful for you every day.

Thank you to **Meg and Molly** my editing ninjas.

Finally, thank you to my adoring husband, **Rob** who literally had to hold my hand through most of this year and cheered me on during this three book series. And to my two children who aren't children anymore, **Luke** and **Haley** who always find time to ask about what I'm writing about in the middle of their own busy lives. I love you all, with all my heart.

Other Books by Kris Calvert

Jane Doe – Scarlett
Jane Doe 2 – Alice
Jane Doe 3 – Catherine

Sex, Lies & Sweet Tea – Book One
Sex, Lies & Lipstick – Book Two
Sex, Lies & Pearls – Book Three
Sex, Lies & Lace – Book Four
Sex, Lies & Bourbon – Book Five
Sex, Lies & Black Tie – Book Six
Sex, Lies & Diamonds – Book Seven – 2018
Sex, Lies & Champagne – Book Eight – 2018
Sex, Lies & Leather – Book Nine – 2018

Beauty

Lead Me From Temptation
Deliver Me From Evil – 2018

Be Mine – a Valentine's Day Novella
Sparks Fly – an Independence Day Novella
Roses are Wrong, Violet's Taboo

Kris Calvert's Website:
www.kriscalvert.com

For Rob

"She burned too bright for this world."

–Emily Brontë, *Wuthering Heights*

DAY ONE | 0600 HOURS

JANE BOARDED THE Acela Express bound for Washington D.C.'s Union Station, taking her single seat in first class. She had no desire to speak or even look at another human and it showed on her sullen face. She'd taken an Ambien and crashed for the first time in days. Sleeping a full eight hours, her body had demanded it. Her mind had fought it with every seed of anxiety and secret turmoil that ran through her scrambled and throbbing head. Years of repressed anger and emotional pain fought its way to the top of her psyche like an angry crowd busting down the entrance to the inner sanctum she'd guarded for years—the place she'd kept under lock and key. A self-preservation tactic, yet now the doors were coming unhinged. So was she. The only cure was to quiet her mind, still her body—sleep.

Ten hours later she was a walking shadow, more dead on the inside than usual, but clinically still the owner of a beating heart.

In her trusty backpack she had what was left of herself: her guns, a change of clothes, duct tape, a copy of Wuthering Heights, a heavy, expandable police file from 1987 that she'd yet to open, a photograph of a man and a scarf owned by the same. It still smelled of him. She still thought of him. And now she was on her way to Washington, D.C. to kill him.

Jane stared out the window into the dark morning, the Acela Express filled to its max capacity. She didn't case the train—her usual routine. She didn't look for a tail, for someone who might be following her. She *knew* her kill assignment—she knew him well. Inside and out. He wasn't following her. He wasn't after her. He wouldn't be a threat. But he *was* an order. And Jane followed orders.

As the express train picked up speed, she ticked through what she really knew. It was the same bits of information she'd run through her busy mind the night before. Without a cipher for the kill assignment, she had no idea as to the *why*, but part of being a soldier is not asking why, but following orders. There were plenty of men Jane could've killed in her previous assignments—men who deserved to die, men who'd killed others or were a threat to kill hundreds or thousands—but she didn't. They weren't her assignment. Not her responsibility. Matt Matthews *was* now Jane's responsibility. She had a job to do—a task.

Last night in the throes of a full-blown panic attack, she ransacked her mind for any and all reasons Coywolf would want him dead. As much as Jane didn't want to admit it, deep down she knew the answer. *Maxtronix.*

Jane had seen with her own eyes the drone in the garage of Six's home in Queens. Matt told her himself he was tracking Three for a story when he was in Atlanta. Still, why had they beat the hell out of him and why did Three order Matt to be killed? It was the *one* piece of the puzzle that didn't fit. And it was the *one* reason Jane continued to fight with herself over the assignment.

In the end she knew what she would do. Jane would follow her order. As her friend who pressed his knee into her chest in the salon told her, it wasn't a matter of *if* they disposed of her, it was a matter of *when*. If Jane knew anything, it was how to take care of herself—take care of number one. She'd accept this last kill assignment and be done. Finished.

After the mission was complete, she would call out of Coywolf on her own, disappear with her police file for a few weeks, and if she could find out who she really was before she left the country, she would at least possess that small tidbit of information to begin her new life.

Gripping her backpack tightly to her chest, Jane could feel the police file in her hands. She didn't know exactly *why* she was unable to open the folder last night. She'd made it as far as sticking her hand inside to feel the stacks upon stacks of papers, but broke down and found herself doing something she'd not done in years—crying.

It was in that moment she decided she couldn't allow that kind of weakness in her life—not now—not yet. When her final kill assignment was complete, she'd open the police file and move on with her life. It was her only incentive to complete the final task. It would be the end of Matt Matthews and the light at the end of a very long, dark tunnel for Jane Doe.

DAY ONE | 0900 HOURS

M ATT MATTHEWS STOPPED at the security gate of his father's estate on the outskirts of Potomac, Maryland. The seven acres that sat on the famous river boasted a sixteen thousand square foot home, tennis courts, pool, pool house, and horse barn. There were ten bedrooms and twelve baths—all for one man. One man who lived alone with his money and the few beautiful women thirty years his junior who would come and go at his pleasure *for* his pleasure.

"Good morning, Mr. Matthews." The security guard greeted Matt with a terse inflection and an even stiffer posture. "Were you expected?"

Matt grimaced. It wasn't the kind of reception he was hoping for after the last twenty-four hours, when he learned of his godfather,

Collie's death. "I don't know if I'm expected or not. But I'm damn sure expecting you to open up this gate and let me pass."

The guard, obviously put out with Matt's comment, picked up the phone in the security house and began to dial. "I'll need to call ahead, sir."

"You know what?" Matt blurted with a mouth full of sarcasm. "Fuck that, I'll call him myself. I can't wait to tell him about the little shit at the security gate who's giving me a *fucking* hard time about getting into my own goddamned house!" The volume in Matt's voice increased with each word that passed over his lips as he pulled his phone from his jacket pocket.

Frantically, the guard waved a hand in the air, dropping the phone receiver onto the cradle with the other. "Hold up, hold up."

The gate lifted. Matt tossed the phone over his shoulder and into the passenger's seat, shaking his head in disgust at the guard as he sped past. "Motherfucker." He called out loud enough for the guard to hear him. Matt didn't care. He was done. Overdone.

He drove the long lane that led to the

circular driveway. The dense green lawns rivaled the lushest golf courses in the world, the gardens more beautiful than even the White House. Christopher Matthews had spared no expense on his homestead when it was built twenty years ago and he only made it more opulent as the profits of Maxtronix continued to grow. Matt couldn't help but get a little sentimental as he pulled up to the front door and parked his old navy BMW. After all, it was here he said goodbye to his mother. It was here he picnicked with her under the shade trees in the backyard. He had some horrible memories of fighting with his father after her death—and even more recently. He loathed the man, but nothing could erase the loving memories he had of his mom. Not even his father.

Past the four white columns on the front of the house, he keyed in his security access code to the estate and heard the lock to the front door click open. Entering the house, the familiar smells of his childhood came back immediately. It was never anything Matt could put his finger on—possibly the wax that had been used on the floors for years, or simply the smell of the African mahogany that graced the walls—the house on the Potomac had a smell all its own and it took Matt back to being a twelve-year-old boy every time he walked through the double doors of the estate. Even if those visits were few and far between.

It was only nine in the morning, but it was a Sunday and if Matt knew one thing about his father, it was that he took his Sunday mornings off very seriously. He suspected he would find the old man on the terrace with a stack of newspapers, an empty breakfast tray and a fresh cup of coffee. He only hoped he wouldn't find a half-dressed leggy blonde on her knees servicing him. It wasn't so far-fetched—it had happened before.

"Dad?" Matt called out through the house, hoping if he was going to interrupt anything he could at least give the woman a chance to get out from under the table.

"Matthew?"

Matt followed the general direction of his father's voice and found him not on the terrace, but in his study in the west wing of the estate.

"Hey," Matt said, upon finding him behind his desk. It was honestly all he could manage in the presence of his father, now knowing everything he'd done and in the wake of Collie's death.

His father looked him up and down, going back to his newspaper immediately. "Didn't expect you today."

Matt hitched his shoulders. "Where else would I go? I don't have an apartment yet. Collie's dead. I wanted to come home."

Christopher Matthews brought only his eyes from the pages of the Sunday New York Times to stare at his son. "I know you're upset, son. I am too."

You really look upset. "Have you heard anything?"

Chris Matthews stood, dropping the newspaper, and walked around his desk to sit on the corner. He crossed his arms. Matt did likewise. "I haven't heard anything. What did you expect to hear?"

If he was killed because of your fucking irresponsibility? That he was killed because you sell our weapons to the militant Islamic State? "Arrangements? When he's being laid to rest at Arlington?"

Matt's father turned and walked back to his chair behind the desk and sat, picking up the paper again. "Tomorrow. Monday," he said before opening the paper again and looking away. "I'd like for you to give the eulogy."

Matt bit down on his lip and held back the string of expletives that were yearning to slip off his tongue with the biting poignancy of a Marine on a bender. "When were you planning on telling me this?"

"Don't get your panties in a wad, Matthew. I've been trying to get in touch with you for days, but the number I have for you is no longer in service. *No one* can seem to get in touch with you, except for maybe *Peter*. I understand you've spoken with *him*," his father said, narrowing his gaze on the paper— seemingly more interested in the close of the market on Friday than the issues at hand.

"I spoke with him about a couple of properties he sent me to look at in Arlington. God knows you don't want me here."

Chris replied, his eyes not leaving the words on the newspaper. "Just because you were a petulant teen the last time you lived here doesn't mean you have to act that way now that you're back for a few days. Let's all try to get along, shall we? Have the cook make you some breakfast and get cleaned up. You look like hell."

Matt stared at this father but didn't reply.

"I know you're upset about Collie," his father continued. "We all are. Take some time to process that today. Write the eulogy. We'll dive headfirst into work on Tuesday." Finally, he dropped his newspaper to take a drink of his coffee. "The new routine will be good for you."

Dumbfounded, Matt stared into his father's face. He wanted to call him an uncaring, unfeeling, piece of shit bastard. He wanted to scream at him and ask him how he could set him up for treason. As an enemy of the United States? How does a man do *that* to his only son? And then he remembered. He remembered how sick his mother had been. How unfeeling his father continued to be. He stared into the face of a man who wasn't a father, but a living, breathing monster.

"Matthew?"

Matt snapped out of his hate-fueled internal rage. If he was going to take down his father, he'd need to keep his head on a swivel and his wits intact. "Sure."

Matt turned and walked out of his father's study and down the long elegant hallway. In his mind he pictured the cocktail parties thrown by his mother. Dozens of people walking about in long dresses and tuxedos while Matthew milled about, mostly hiding under the silk chiffon of his mother's beautiful gowns. She would smile and send him up the staircase. The same steps Matt now climbed one by one. It was a sweet and yet painful memory. It was troublesome to think of how wonderful it once was—what could've been. For now, Matt would go to the same room he'd retreated to as a child—his own—and do as he did back then. Devise a way out of the trouble he was in.

DAY ONE | 0930 HOURS

IN THE MIDDLE of the crime scene, Sergeant Kelly Casey stared at the peeling wallpaper in the Queens, N.Y. house. A wall filled with photographs of men on the FBI's terror watch list—on NYPD's terrorist list. A lackey from the FBI began taking everything down for evidence—all of it. All dead, the photos were a shrine to those who'd given their lives for the cause. Kelly shifted his weight and shook his head. There seemed to be something missing— *someone* missing—right in the middle. It was as if a photo had been removed from the shrine, from the *center* of the shrine.

Walking through the house in Queens owned by Saanen Al-Sistani, Kelly kept a low profile. A suspected member of a terror group with ties to ISIS, the very short and rotund man was now dead and lying in the city morgue.

Kelly wasn't mad about it. One less thing to worry about. It was *how* he died that bothered him more than the fact that he was dead.

The house, still full of investigators, had been cleared out by the FBI, but nobody was going to tell Kelly Casey to get out of his own crime scene. *No one.*

"Hey boss, did you get a load of what they found in the garage?"

Kelly didn't say anything. He preferred to keep a low profile. Especially while the Feds were running around like schoolchildren during recess. Instead he nodded. He'd seen the military drone. It'd left him with a pit in his stomach the size of Yankee Stadium. They'd trained to counteract drones over the skies of New York, but Kelly never thought he'd live to see the day when one would actually make it into the city—and an American made drone at that. Someone at Maxtronix had some explaining to do.

The entire house had been brushed for prints. There was nothing there but those of Al-Sistani and his crew. What Kelly was most interested in was the prints on the remote control of the helicopter—the helicopter that crushed the known terrorist's neck and nearly severed his head. Interestingly enough, there were barely *any* prints on the controls.

It didn't add up. None of it. And yet to Kelly, it did.

Out the front door, Kelly walked the perimeter of the house. Noting the tall fence, he knew the activity that took place in the back was completely obscured. Back on the sidewalk, he thought of his conversation with Alice on the front stoop and envisioned the tiny blood splatters on her jacket all over again. He stared at his feet on the sidewalk and looked up, squinting in the sunlight. He didn't want to believe it, but still, he couldn't shake the thought from his mind.

Looking behind him, Kelly counted the black cars. He'd never seen evidence moved out of a scene so fast. Across the street, an older man sitting on the front steps of the Methodist church watched. It was still early, and Sunday service wouldn't begin for another hour and a half, but the front doors were open and ready to greet those who wanted to worship. Kelly popped his brow, looked both ways and crossed over.

People in Queens were neighborhood folk. They liked to sit on their stoops and chat. None of the next door neighbors seemed to know anything. To Kelly, it was worth a shot.

"Hey there." Kelly put his hand up, but didn't wave. "How's it going?"

Lenny Lee, head deacon of the church, was dressed in a suit that looked too big for him. He nodded, but didn't reply.

"You been watching all this go down across the street?"

"Who wants to know?" Lenny asked.

Kelly pulled his badge, flashed it. "I'm Sergeant Casey, NYPD."

"Youse know who killed the guy?"

Kelly took a seat on the church steps next to him. "We're working on it. Were you here yesterday, around eleven or so in the morning?"

Lenny nodded.

"Inside? Outside?"

"I work in the flowers on the nice days. I'm a deacon here at the church. I'm Lenny. Lenny Lee."

"It's nice to meet you, Mr. Lee. So you were *outside*?"

Lenny nodded again.

"Did you happen to see anything?"

A strange look overcame Lenny and he dropped his chin to his chest before shaking off his irritation.

"What?"

"I don't really...I don't remember."

Kelly stood and faced Lenny, blocking the sun to get a better look at him. "I don't follow. What do you mean, you don't remember?"

Lenny shrugged. "I was planting like I always do. I like the flowers to look good on Sundays. Anyways, I find her back here and then I don't remember a fuckin' thing. 'Scuse me. Sorry. But I don't remember."

The corner of Kelly's mouth curled up in anticipation. "*Her*?"

Lenny dropped his chin to his chest. "I dunno. I thought she was a runaway. She looked like a kid to me—wearing her hoodie and the headphones and all."

"Five seven, five-eight? One ten? Brown hair, blondish streaks? Blue eyes." By the time Kelly got to the end of his description, he was no longer asking. He was certain by the expression painted on Lenny's face they were discussing the same woman.

"That's her. I tried to feed her the other day, but she wasn't havin' it."

"Wait," Kelly said putting his hand in the air. "You mean she's been here more than once? Before yesterday?"

Lenny nodded. "Couple days before that. Then yesterday. But like I said, I don't remember anything. I woke up in the flowers back there like I'd been drinking all day and I've been sober fifteen years. It's a terrible thing to wake up and not know what the hell's goin' on, you know?"

Kelly stepped back, placing his hands on his hips. He traded glances between Lenny and the house across the street. "Yeah, I know, man. I know. Listen," Kelly dug into his back pocket for a business card and handed it to Lenny. "This is my number. If you think of anything else, and I mean *anything* about her, you call me."

"I've told you everything."

"Keep the card anyway."

Lenny held it in the air, as if to say thank you, then tucked it in the front pocket of his gaping suit coat.

"Sergeant Casey!" A young cop called out

from the house across the street.

Kelly looked behind him, then pointed to Lenny, issuing a thank you and goodbye without saying a word. He crossed the street, meeting the officer and his crew at the edge of the house.

"Sir. You're not gonna believe what we just found in the basement."

"After today, I think I'd believe anything."

"Sir, the FBI's just called in the Army Chemical Corps. There's fucking *sarin gas* in the *fucking* basement of this *fucking* house."

"Sarin *where?*" Kelly felt compelled to ask the question even though he'd clearly heard the location.

The young officer lowered his voice as the men and women inside the house began pouring out. "There's a stockpile of it wrapped in rugs in the basement, sir. They're clearing the house. And then they're clearing the neighborhood."

Kelly only had two words. "Fuck. Me."

DAY ONE | 1200 HOURS

JANE RANG THE bell on the counter of the Rustic Virginian Motel on the Potomac River. An elderly lady wearing an old-fashioned gingham house dress and pink slippers shuffled from a back room to greet her at the reception desk. Jane thought if her hair had been in rollers, she could've been a cartoon character, but instead, she wore a bad wig. An unlit cigarette hung from her pursed lips, her glasses perched at the tip of her nose. Hunched over, her feet never left the ground as she skated them one in front of the other.

"Sorry honey," she said. "I don't move as fast as I used to."

Jane gave her a fleeting upturn of her mouth, but said nothing.

"You need a room?"

Jane nodded and the older woman stopped

to take a better look at her. "You speak English?" she asked, raising her voice.

"Yes."

The lady bobbled her head. "Oh, okay. I was just making sure you were understanding me. It's eighty dollars a day—ninety if you want maid service every day."

"No."

"Do you want to pay with a credit card or—"

"Cash," Jane said, cutting her off at the pass. "I'm going to be here a week. I'd like to pay in advance."

"A week in advance is fine," she replied, taking the cigarette from her lips and placing it on the ledge of the counter as if it were burning. "What do you want to do about clean sheets and towels?"

"I'll be fine with the sheets for a week. Can I pick up and drop off towels at the front desk?"

The woman twisted her face and drew her head back into her neck as if she'd never heard the question in her life. "I suppose. So you don't want anyone cleaning your room? At all?"

Jane shook her head.

"You ain't turning tricks in my motel are you?" she asked, placing a hand-written registry on the counter. " 'Cause I can't have that going on. We've had trouble with some of the new people in Washington thinking they can come in here and tear up the place and have a *sex-shu-al* free-for-all."

Jane blinked deliberately. And although she admired the way the old woman butchered the word *sexual*, her face remained stoic—her body rigid. "No."

"If you're paying cash, I'm gonna need you to sign the register. Between you, me and the fence post, I don't care what name you write down, but I have to have something. You can write, Jane Doe for all I care."

Jane blanched at the sound of her own name, then ignored the pen in the woman's hand, and procured one from her own backpack. She signed the register, citing her hometown as Yorkshire, NY.

"Catherine Bell, welcome to the Rustic Virginian. Room number three is all yours."

She took the retro fob attached to the room key. Engraved in the plastic was the number 3. Jane couldn't help but raise an eyebrow at the irony.

"Don't lose the key."

Jane nodded.

"And keep it down. We have a lot of older people who stay here on the weekends. They don't like loud music."

Jane said nothing.

The old lady pointed to the backpack Jane carried in her right hand and the Walgreens bag in her left. "That all the luggage you got, sweetie?"

Jane didn't answer the question, merely backed out of the lobby door, holding her hand in the air to say goodbye.

Outside, Jane looked left and right. The Rustic Virginian was a twelve room motel with the rooms splitting in the center of the lobby. Rooms one thru six ran from the right side to the east end. Room seven to twelve from the left of the lobby to the west end. Jane's room was on the end of the building, just where she liked it.

She looked at the other five rooms on her way to her own. It seemed only rooms One and Two were occupied, but it was hard to tell. All the curtains were drawn and if the lights weren't on, it was difficult to discern if anyone was home. It was a perfect spot for Jane to hang out for a few days.

Letting herself in, the first thing she noticed was the smell—mold. On her trip to a big box store, air freshener was on the top of the list.

Jane turned on the lamp by the bed and walked around the room to inspect it carefully. In the bathroom she checked the window over the tub, making sure it opened. She wanted a way out of the motel room other than the front door if she needed it. Sadly, for this assignment, no one would be watching her. She knew her target. He didn't carry a gun. He couldn't even fight for his own life. Matt Matthews was a sitting duck.

Jane dumped her backpack and the contents of her drugstore shopping bag onto the bed. A bottle of blonde hair coloring and a new burner phone lay on the faded bedspread. She looked at herself in the dingy yellow lighting of the shabby motel and started peeling off her clothes. Taking the boxed hair color in her grip, she opened her backpack and searched until she found what she needed—her knife.

Into the bathroom she walked, hoping the

lighting would be better. The old plastic fixture had a green hue to it as mildew from years of moisture in the ancient tiled room had turned the light into a Petri dish. Jane climbed on the toilet seat and pried it off, revealing a forty-watt bulb that cast the white light she needed.

With a click, she opened her switchblade, shook out her newly highlighted mane and systematically began to hack her hair to her shoulders. Taking small sections into her grip at a time, she did her best to keep it somewhat even. "Sorry Lance," Jane said aloud as she cringed at the thought of the prissy man, just forty-five minutes away in his fancy hair salon who'd done such a nice job cutting and highlighting her hair. She wouldn't be nearly as precise or artistic.

Bit by bit, she whacked away—disconnected—far from the reality of what she was doing to herself. When she finished, Jane's hair lay in pieces on the floor. She mixed the bottle blonde as prescribed and squeezed the contents over her head, careful not to get it in her eyes. Checking the instructions, she looked to her watch and set the time. She'd have to wait forty-five minutes to become another person—again.

The new burner phone lay on the pilled and discolored bedspread. She picked it up and turned it on, then sat on the edge of the bed, wrapping one of the threadbare towels from the bathroom around her shoulders as the hair bleach began to drip like melting ice cream onto her shoulders.

Dialing, she looked to the clock radio on the nightstand that flickered every third second or so. Jane assumed someone who didn't want to get out of bed one hungover morning on the banks of the Potomac decided to toss the alarm clock across the room. Now it blinked like a nervous one-eyed cat.

The line rang on the other end. When the fourth ring came, Jane thought about ending the call. She wouldn't leave a message.

"Hello?"

His voice was faint and hoarse. It gave Jane a worrisome knot in the pit of her stomach. It'd only been a week and a half since she'd spoken with him last, but even days seemed to take their toll on the priest who kept her secret. "Father Doheny? It's me."

"Hello, my child. I was just thinking about

you this morning. Praying for you. How are you?"

"I'm…" Jane looked at herself in the faded mirror across from the bed in the rundown motel. Her eyes had sunken into her head and were now surrounded by dark circles. Her once dark and silky mane was now merely a mess of bleach burning her scalp, her hair now hacked into sections that more closely resembled straw. She was weary, hungry and frankly, lost. "I'm fine."

"Why am I not convinced you're being truthful with me?"

Jane sighed, turning away from the mirror. She couldn't stand the sight of her own reflection. "Because you know me too well."

"I know you well enough to understand you call only when you are looking for guidance."

An insignificant, guilty smile passed across Jane's lips. Father Doheny knew her better than anyone—at least better than anyone who was still alive. She swallowed hard.

"What is it?" he asked. "Speak up. I'm an old man, you know."

"Father, I think I have the police file from

the night I was found in the dumpster in Pittsburgh."

"What do you mean, you think?"

"I met a man, a New York City police officer. His father was a cop in Pittsburgh. He told me this story of his dad finding a baby in a dumpster twenty-nine years ago. It was an unsolved case that haunted him. Anyway, his father retired and has since passed away."

"And?"

"His father made a copy of the police file and his son had the file."

"And his son gave it to you?"

Jane bit her lip. "Not exactly."

"What do you mean, *not exactly*?"

"I took it."

"Took it, how?"

An awkward silence filled the phone line. Jane could hear Father Doheny breathing on the other end and it made her highly uncomfortable. She'd always been truthful with the priest—always. There was no reason to start lying to him now. "I stole it from the wall safe in his apartment after lifting the keys from his car."

More silence.

"Father?"

"I'm still here. I'm just wondering why you had to steal."

"Why do I do anything I do, Father? Because it's necessary."

"The only thing necessary in life, my child, is to believe and repent. The rest is in God's hands."

"That might work for you, Father, but I have things I have to do in this world. In case you haven't noticed, God hasn't always been there to help me out. I've been balling on my own most of my life."

"God never promises life will be easy. He promises he will never leave you."

"Really? Because I've felt left."

"I don't know how many times we have to discuss this for you to understand it, but you are on this earth for a reason, child. You've been saved, by the grace of God—I might add—too many times. You've saved, dare I say, thousands of lives with the work you've done. I think that's a pretty fine statistic if you ask me, but back to the matter at hand. You've taken something that doesn't belong to you."

"How is a file *about me*, not belong to *me*?"

"No matter what, you must promise that you will get what belongs to this police officer back into his hands. Promise me."

Jane cracked her neck, sending hair bleach flying onto the already stained carpet and let out a loud sigh. "Fine. You have my word. I'll get the file back to him. *Somehow*."

"Good. Now, is that the only reason you called?"

Jane hesitated. "No."

"I'm listening."

"I want out. I want out for good. I don't know what *it* is anymore. I'm just…"

"Weary?"

"Maybe."

"I've been asked to do something—"

"This is something you don't *wish* to do."

"It's an order, Father. It doesn't matter what I think about it. I follow orders. That's what an order is."

"But you're questioning it."

"I'm not here to question orders."

"Then why are you calling me?"

Jane fell silent. The bleach on her head was burning her scalp beyond what she could tolerate. Either that, or Father Doheny's words were beyond what she could listen to. It was time to wash it out. It was time to hang up. "I don't know. I don't know anything anymore."

"Come home. Come home to Pittsburgh. Leave all of this behind and start anew. It's been your goal—your plan. To be quite honest, I can't hold out much longer, Jane. It's time for me to rest as well. I've waited as long as I can for you, but if you take too long…"

Jane stood at his words. "Don't say it, Father."

"I'm not trying to—"

"No, I know. I understand. And I will. I'll be in Pittsburgh soon. I need to finish this. For my own life."

"Good."

"Take care, Father."

"I do. I pray for you, my child—every day."

"It's what keeps me alive."

"*God* keeps you alive. *You* keep you alive. Come home alive."

Jane hung up without saying goodbye. It was too hard. She knew Father Doheny was right—she knew because his words cut through her like a knife.

Jane walked back to the bathroom and

started the shower. Taking the towel from her shoulders, she could see in the mirror how blonde her hair had become—even *with* the bleach still dripping from her head.

Jane slipped the jeans from her thin frame and unhooked her bra, sliding behind the see-thru shower curtain. The water was hot and the pressure strong. She lathered up her body with the tiny sliver of paper covered soap from housekeeping and rinsed the caustic and burning bleach from her hair, shampooing with the samples left behind by the last guest.

In and out in ten minutes, Jane stepped from the tub, towel drying her hair as she wiped the fog from the bathroom mirror. Jane Doe was now officially a blue-eyed blonde.

DAY ONE | 1400 HOURS

KELLY CASEY STOOD in front of Majestic Rugs at Thirty-Eighth and Eighth Avenue in Midtown Manhattan. It wasn't the inside of the building where Al-Sistani's uncle or the other two young jihadis were found with the female slaves that bothered him—he felt bad enough the operation was going on right under their noses and no one was the wiser. It wasn't even the way Al-Sistani's uncle was tied to the chair or the Arabic message left on his forehead in permanent marker. It was the surgical precision with which the tasks were carried out. Even the women who'd been rescued refused to speak of the angel who'd saved their lives.

Kelly walked the alleyway between the fabric store and rug shop looking for something—anything. There were a few footprints that had been marked as evidence, but even those seemed to match the men who'd since been taken to the hospital or into custody—not the so called *angel*.

"What am I missing?" he said aloud, leaning his left shoulder into the decaying brick to stare across the way at the all-night diner. Then, remembering his chat with Lenny at the church just that morning, he crossed the street.

The bell rang out over the door and Sergeant Casey put on his best smile as he approached the lunch counter. "Hi."

"Hello," the waitress replied. "What can I do for you?"

Kelly leaned into the counter, his black leather jacket rubbing against itself and his hard muscles as he reached for his badge. "I'm Sergeant Kelly Casey and I was wondering," he said, nodding his head to the store across the street without losing eye contact with the attentive waitress. "Have you noticed anything suspicious going on over there? Or anyone here in the diner watching the store? Maybe asking questions about it?"

The waitress was in her mid-thirties and looked as if she'd worked the overnight shift, but was pulling a double against her will. She glanced across the street at the storefront, now closed and roped off with police tape, then looked back to Kelly. "Maybe. Why?"

Kelly popped his chin in affirmation. "Do you have a moment? I'd like to ask you some questions."

The waitress made a face. It was clear she didn't want to get involved. At the same time, she looked like death walking and perhaps needed a moment off her feet. "Is your boss around? I'm happy to ask him if you can take a break."

"Roy?" she called over her shoulder and into the kitchen.

"Yeah?"

"I'm taking my break. Someone's here from NYPD. Wants to ask me a couple questions about the rug place across the street."

Roy stuck his head out from under the stainless steel order wheel and barked, "What the hell do you know about that, Martha?"

"Keep your pants on, Roy. It's time for my break anyway."

"This is official police business, sir. Do you have a problem with that? Because I don't have a problem with calling my buddies at the Health

Department to make a surprise inspection."

"Fuck you," Roy murmured under his breath. "Take all the damn time you need."

"Coffee?" she asked with a smile, pointing to the booth by the window.

"Sure," Kelly replied.

"Cream? Sugar?"

"Yes and yes."

"Have a seat. I'll bring it right out."

Kelly walked to the booth, sitting down to stare out the window. It was the perfect place to case the rug store. Kelly could almost see her sitting there. Watching. Waiting.

When Martha slid in, she startled him. "Sorry," she said. "You were somewhere else."

Kelly shook his head. "Just thinking."

"Here," she said, sliding his mug of coffee across the table along with a sugar caddie and two small Carnation half and half creamer cups. "Sorry. We don't have real cream. Roy's too cheap."

"This is great. I need a pick me up."

Martha sipped her coffee and smiled. "Me too."

Kelly poured in the creamer and tossed in two sugars before he began his interrogation.

Stirring his coffee, he sat the spoon on the paper napkin and took a sip. "Mmmm. Good coffee."

"I made it," she replied.

Kelly leaned back in the seat, laying his arm across the back of the booth. "How long you been working here?

"A year."

"You work mostly nights or days?"

"Mostly nights. I audition during the days. I'm an actress. Right now mostly off-off Broadway stuff, but I'm hopeful, you know?"

Kelly nodded. "Sure. So have you noticed—"

"You want to know what I've seen going on over there?" she asked, pointing across her chest to the rug shop.

Kelly shrugged his shoulders. "Maybe."

"Oh," she said. "I just assumed."

"I'm really more interested in what's been going on in here."

"What do you mean?"

"I mean, did anyone come in on a regular basis and sit? Maybe in one of these booths along the window and just, you know, *watch* the rug store?"

Kelly watched Martha sip her coffee and think through his question. She took a deep breath and chewed on her bottom lip. "I mean, *maybe*. There was this one girl."

Kelly sat up in his seat. "A girl?"

Martha nodded into her mug of coffee. "She didn't eat anything. Just looked at her laptop a lot and drank a little coffee. Mostly she just sat. Watched. She was a good tipper."

"Did she by chance use a credit card?" Kelly asked the question, but already knew the answer.

Martha shook her head. "Cash only. She always wore this zip-up gray hoodie too. And her headphones. I don't know what she listened too, but she must've really liked it."

"Why do you say that?"

"She never took the earbuds out. Even when she was talking to me. I dunno. Maybe she wasn't listening to anything at all."

Kelly nodded, encouraging Martha to share more. "Did she ever ask you any questions about the rug shop?"

Martha shook her head. "She just watched it. I told her some stuff. I mean, obviously she was interested. Look, I know I'm just a waitress, but I can read people pretty good, ya know?

She was into what was going on over there."

"What exactly did you tell her?"

"That I didn't know why they made such a big fuss over the big rolling security gate."

"What do you mean?"

"Every morning, those guys?" Martha said pointing across the street. "They would fight over the security gate. I mean, who knows what they were really saying to each other, but it wasn't good. Just a lot of pointing to the gate and each other."

"Why do you think they fought?"

Martha shrugged. "I dunno. It's like I told her, they came and went at all hours of the night through the *back door*. I told her I thought they were living there."

"Why?"

"Why what?"

"Why would you think they were living there?"

Martha's eyes got big and she shrugged her shoulders, over exaggerating her suspicions. "I don't know, maybe because they were dragging women in and out at all hours of the night. I had a customer come in one day who complained about how bad it smelled in there. I just put two and two together, you know?"

Kelly nodded. "So what exactly did you tell the woman who was sitting in the booth?"

"I told her what I just told you. I think people live inside there. That they come and go thru the alley door all night and that it smells. And you know what?"

"What?"

"I was right."

Kelly nodded. He couldn't fault her. She *was* right. She'd also confirmed what he suspected. Alice had been hard at work inside the Majestic Rug store and she'd left a message on the forehead of Al-Sistani's uncle. But why?

"Thanks, Martha," Kelly said, sliding out of the booth. Reaching into his jacket pocket, he pulled out a business card. "If you think of anything else—*anything*—give me a call."

Martha stood and met him, taking the card from his hand. She nodded. "Okay."

Kelly dropped a five onto her table before stepping out onto Thirty-Eighth Street. He paused. Alice had been at both crime scenes and knew *exactly* what she was doing. But she'd been dealing with amateurs and sloppy jihadis. Kelly Casey was neither.

DAY ONE | 1600 HOURS

SITTING IN THE chair where he'd studied for every test he'd ever taken in middle school, Matt stared at the photograph on his desk. He was no more than fifteen years old in the picture. Collie looked to be in his sixties, but military men always looked younger than they really were to Matt. It was the fitness of their body, the nature of their posture and badass character. Their attitude never got old and it never seemed to age the soldier either. "Collie, what happened?" he asked under his breath. Matt had spent the better part of the afternoon going through old photos and memories, beating himself up over the events of the past two years—beating himself up over the events of the past *two weeks*.

His old room looked virtually the same as it had the day he left for college in Pittsburgh. His various sports trophies lined the walls along with a few creative writing awards and the journalism award from his high school newspaper. There were prom pictures, photos of spring break and even a few baby pictures—Matt with his mother in the swing that hung from the great oak tree on the back of the property and even Matt cooking in the kitchen with her. But there were no pictures of Matt Matthews and his father. They weren't close, never had been, and neither seemed to care.

Being back in the house with his father brought up too many unresolved issues for Matt to feel any calming presence or sense of home. The huge estate *wasn't* home. Home for Matt was his condo in Pittsburgh. The one *he'd* bought and paid for. The place he'd not been in over a year—the place he'd probably never return to.

He sat back in the oak chair, the antique wood moaning under his weight. In front of him was the blinking white page of a document on his MacBook. He'd not written one word of Collie's eulogy. Zero. The blank page stared at him, taunting him. He was a writer with no words for the man who meant the most to him of anyone in his life. When he couldn't take the lack of meaningful sentences mocking him any longer, he shut the laptop in frustration and stood, whipping his leather jacket around his shoulders and cramming his arms through the sleeves as he rushed about the bedroom collecting the keys to his BMW and his sunglasses.

Dashing down the grand staircase, he noticed the lights in the front entry were on—the imposing crystal chandelier twinkled not only from the bulbs, but also from the direct sunlight now shining through the large western facing window. Glancing down the long hallway, he spied his father pacing inside his office and dictating his email. The man could run a billion-dollar company, but he couldn't type for shit.

Matt walked out the front door without saying goodbye or telling a single staff person he was leaving, although he suspected everyone would eventually know. Nothing went on at his father's estate that Christopher Matthews *wasn't* privy to. *Nothing.*

Matt's car was still parked in the circular driveway, as he'd refused to give up his keys earlier to one of the many butlers who'd wanted to move it to a garage. Matt didn't like being at the house in Potomac in the first place, but for now it was necessary. Still, as long as he was there, he wanted his *stuff* to stay out of his father's hands and therefore *out* of his garage.

Roaring up the long lane that lead to the security gate, he was met by a new guard. "Leaving, sir?"

Matt nodded.

"Coming back?"

"Only because I have to." Matt said it as a joke, but it was the truth.

"I'm working late tonight, sir. I'll be here when you return."

Matt gave him a thumbs up.

The gate opened slowly and Matt pulled through, taking only a moment to ensure no one was on the tiny highway before peeling out of the driveway. He needed to clear his head. To go somewhere. Anywhere. Anywhere but where he was.

Rolling down the windows, Matt let the air fill his car. He had less than twenty-four hours to think of what to say tomorrow at the foot of Collie's grave. How did he stand in front of a crowd of people who loved and respected a man of such greatness and say, *it was my fault?* Matt wanted Collie's death to have been a natural occurrence, but he wasn't convinced it was true.

Matt fidgeted in his seat as the BMW accelerated. He glanced in his rearview mirror. The blue xenon headlights of a nondescript black SUV caught his eye. He was being followed. For how long, he didn't know. Quickly crossing two lanes to take an off ramp, Matt caused a minivan and a small convertible to lock up their brakes, honk and throw up hand gestures. He didn't care. The SUV followed.

"Shit."

There was only one place Matt knew he could go where the tail couldn't follow—Max HQ. Making a U-turn at the next light, Matt sped in and out of cars, hitting the brakes in between lane changes, causing bits of paper and his field bag to fly from the front seat of his car and onto the floorboard. Running a red light and putting four cars and more than a few frazzled drivers between them, he tried to ditch the SUV, taking the freeway, speeding to headquarters in Arlington. No matter the maneuver, the black car followed, causing two cars to crash. It meant one thing—it wasn't an amateur driving—it was an alphabet agent on his tail. FBI, CIA, NSA—someone who wouldn't have to answer for their actions. Someone he didn't want to deal with. Flooring the accelerator, he topped out at ninety miles per hour, praying for a speed trap and a veteran cop *without* a sense of humor. It didn't happen. He focused his attention on the road, weaving in and out of cars and doing his best to keep the others around him safe. Unlike the tail behind him, he would have to answer for any havoc he might wreak. He hadn't been trained to drive NASCAR. Matt was literally flying by the seat of his pants.

Finally reaching the Arlington exit that led to Maxtronix headquarters, he passed three cars on the wrong side of the road when the opportunity presented itself, and opened up the throttle down the service road to the edge of the company property.

The first security booth sat at the edge of the wooded area that was the fifty-four acre Maxtronix campus. His brakes screaming to a halt, he frantically pulled the security badge from the floor of his car and waved his credentials at the booth. "Open the fucking gate. Now!"

Without hesitation, security parted the massive double iron gates. Matt drove through before it completely opened, speeding toward the main building at seventy miles per hour. In his rearview mirror, he could see the black SUV come to a grinding halt and park on the street, idling. Two armed company guards walked to the gate as it closed, gripping their AR-15s.

"Motherfucker. Who are you?" Matt asked under his breath, hunching down in the seat to get a better look at the car as he distanced himself. Turning at the end of the lane, Matt drove to the parking spot that now bore his name.

Out of the car and out of sight, he cracked his neck, releasing the tension he'd built in the last twenty minutes. Climbing the steps two by two, he entered the building, giving a wave to the weekend security guard.

Matt still had the new credentials he'd been given on his last visit to Max HQ in his sweaty grip—the visit where he'd told his father he was joining the ranks of the company—aligning with the Maxtronix Team—the twisted, money-grubbing, treasonous, enemy-colluding team of war mongers. It wasn't who he *ever* wanted to be and yet here he was, more a part of it now than ever.

The thirty billion dollar defense contractor and war drone manufacturer to the U.S. Military wasn't the patriotic company they proposed to be, but instead nothing more than a dirty, cheap profiteering group, trading their goods to the highest bidder. And in Matt's case, to the Islamic State, to the tune of six hundred and seventy-six million dollars. And thanks to his father, all in his name. Traded for oil in the Middle East, Matt was the proud owner of millions of barrels of crude, all of which had been sold and the cash placed in a Trust—*his* Trust.

Now, fifty-two deadly drones were in the hands of extremists. Drones armed with artillery capable of taking out hundreds of people in pinpoint target areas were in the possession of those who wished to do nothing more than to end the culture of the West and fly their flag from the top of the Capitol just a few miles from where Matthew stood in

Virginia.

Matt climbed aboard the elevator and swiped his credentials again. He headed straight for his late grandfather's office. He hoped whomever had been charged with the task of refitting it to meet his needs as a new vice president had not had the time or inclination in the past week to get much done. Matt wanted to sit at his grandfather's desk—feel his Gran around him—search for answers from the man he so admired and respected.

The elevator stopped not at the top floor— the place from which Christopher Matthews ruled his kingdom, but one floor below. It was the floor of V.P.'s, a place his father rarely came down from his throne room to visit. The vice presidents were summoned to the tower to meet the King. Matt knew how that felt. He'd been dealing with it his entire life.

The elevator opened with a loud ring. Matt took one step off and stood toe to toe with Dr. Peter Hudson.

For decades, Peter had been Christopher Matthew's head of research and development. A brilliant man, he was also Chris Matthew's whipping boy—the whipping boy who'd come to Matt's aid by risking everything to show him the business transactions between his father and the Islamic State.

"Jesus. Thank God you're here."

"Keep your voice down," Peter said, taking him by the arm to lead him down the hallway.

"You're not going to believe what just happened to me."

Peter shook his head, silently asking Matt to stop talking. Picking up the pace, he led him off the floor and into a stairwell. Down six flights they went in silence until Matt opened his mouth once again and asked, "What are you doing?"

Peter held up a finger, stopping on the third floor of the building to swipe them both onto the floor and out of the concrete encased tower of steps. Four more security swipes through doors and parts of Maxtronix Matt never knew existed and Peter finally let go of his arm and took a seat behind a tall lab desk and a bank of computers. When the door behind them shut, an airlock system took all the breath from the room. It was silent—soundproof.

Matt could hear himself breathing—his

heart pounding in his chest. "Where the hell are we?"

"We're in a secluded lab location inside Maxtronix. It's soundproof and debugged. You're safe here. *I'm* safe here."

"What the…?"

"Look Matt, I've known for some time now that your father couldn't be trusted. General Collins came to me. Your grandfather's company needed to be saved from itself—from your father—from destruction. There's a hell of a lot of good that goes on here. No one, including me, wanted to see their hard work go to waste or worse, fall into the wrong hands. With the help of General Collins, we took some measures before your grandfather passed away to insure that you would have something to inherit."

"You mean Gran didn't trust his own son?"

Dr. Peter Hudson was a brilliant man. A skilled PhD in engineering, biology, physics and chemistry. What he didn't have was the capacity to deliver information with tact. Facts were his forte. "Matthew, your father never cared much about anything but himself and money. Your grandfather knew it, your mother knew it.

Megalomania is fine for a delusional man with no means, but couple it with access to weapons of destruction and you have a recipe for disaster. Your grandfather feared it, Collie understood it—and now, unfortunately, you've come to realize it."

They were harsh words—but true words all the same. "I was followed here, Peter. Black SUV. Probably government. I—" Matt stopped short of coming clean with Peter about the past two years and the work he'd been doing in the Middle East. There was no reason to involve the man in anything more than he was already completely tangled in.

"There's no time for that, Matthew. I have a plan."

"You—*you*—" Matt stuttered through his words. "Have a plan?"

Peter nodded. "Follow me."

Matt followed Peter through a series of pressurized doors, each one needing a different type of security key to enter. The first, facial recognition.

Placing his chin on a perch, Peter remained still as the biometric scanner searched for tiny traits and attributes found only on Peter

Hudson's face. The pressurized doors opened and they proceeded down another hallway and two more flights of stairs.

The second was a retinal device. Peter placed his eye in front of the small scanner. "Where? How?"

Matt's astonishment at how something so big was hiding right in the heart of Maxtronix Global HQ was apparent—and right under his father's nose. Chris Matthews—the man who knew every move everyone around him was making, was clueless. Matt was certain of it.

Peter waved him inside the second door, asking him to follow without answering.

Finally, the third door was a vein authentication key. Utilizing the unique pattern of veins underneath the surface of Peter's skin as he flexed his fingers, it was impossible to replicate. The complete architecture of the blood vessels in Peter's entire right hand was the key and he had to be alive, totally conscious and moving his fingers in order for the scan to work. Severing his hand or dragging his lifeless or unconscious body to the locked door wouldn't work.

"*Dr. Hudson!*" Matt exclaimed as he

watched in awe as the software read the pattern of blood pulsing through the man's veins and capillaries. Peter remained stoic and calm, urging Matt to follow him.

"Jesus, Peter," Matt sighed as he followed him into the secret research and development laboratory. "How long have you been working back here?"

"Long enough."

"What have you been working *on*?"

"Plenty, but for now, we need to worry about how to destroy the drones that are in the hands of those who mean to do us harm."

"Do we even know where they are?"

"They're all equipped with a tracking system. I *can* find them."

"Then what? We send in more drones? Legit U.S. forces to destroy them?"

Peter shook his head slowly.

"I'm not following. Because any way you look at it, I'm screwed," Matt said taking a seat in one of the tall chairs tucked under a lab station.

"All of these are equipped with a suicide pill preloaded into their mainframe," Peter explained, pointing to three detailed drone blueprints hanging on an adjacent wall. "Just like a good old fashioned cyanide pill taken by a spy to keep from being captured and tortured to give up their secrets, the drones we send out into the world are equipped with the same. Anything shot down or captured needs to self-destruct. Why would we ever want anyone with our technology in their hands?"

Matt became almost giddy. "So that's it. We just find them and blow them. It's over." Grabbing his head with both hands, he stood and squeezed his face, squatting to the floor before slamming his open palms to the ground in triumph.

"Matt." Peter's voice was calm. He wasn't celebrating. "*Matthew.*"

"What?" Matt stood and paced the room. He looked as though the weight of the world had been lifted from his shoulders.

"It's not that simple."

"What do you mean? You just said."

Peter shook his head. "There's a sequence of numbers—an encryption. It's a failsafe—all a part of drone risk mitigation. We need the second part of the sequence in order to set the self-destruct mechanism into action."

"So?" Matt asked raising his hand in the air, still too excited to find a problem with the plan.

"The first set of the sequence is held by command. The second set of numbers is held by the operator of the war drone. Not just one, but both sets of numbers must be used. Not one of the two can set it off on their own."

"I'm not following."

"When your father sold these machines to the Islamic State, there was no failsafe in place. We have the first set of sequence numbers because we built the machines," Peter explained.

Matt sat in the nearest chair. The wind had quickly left his sails. "We don't have the second set."

Peter shook his head. "No."

Matt bit his lip, crossing his arms over his chest. "Any chance in that money trail of oil trading there could be a name—someone to whom Dad might have passed that information?"

Peter cleared his throat. "We have only one man."

"And?"

"Siad al Daleel ul Khyayraat."

DAY ONE | 2100 HOURS

KELLY CASEY STEPPED into the Time Flies Café and was immediately met by the hostess, Star. "Well hello there, my red-headed brother. Can I get you a table for a late dinner?" she asked, batting fake eyelashes matted with the blue shadow she'd caked on earlier in the day.

Kelly smoothed back his own natural red hair with one hand and inspected the diner. He wasn't interested in eating. "I'm Sergeant Casey, NYPD," he said flashing his badge. "I was wondering if the owner was around."

Vincent *Vegas* Kowalski came from behind the counter, wiping his hands in perfect rhythm with each step he took. "I'm the owner. What can I do for you?"

Kelly put his hand out for a shake and gave the older man with the long grey ponytail the once-over. "Kelly Casey."

"Yeah, NYPD. I heard."

"Is there some place we can talk?"

The cheap redhead and the tiny girl also behind the counter watched every move Kelly made with their boss as he ushered the cop to a booth in the back. "Can I get you a cup of coffee or something?"

Kelly shook his head. "I just need a moment of your time. Want to ask you a few questions, Mr.?"

"Vincent…Kowalski. Everybody calls me Vegas."

Kelly unapologetically raised a single cynical eyebrow. "*Vegas?*"

Vegas looked away as if he was already guilty. "Yeah…it's a nickname," he replied, dropping his voice. "'Cause I'm lucky."

"Ah."

"Hope it's not gonna run out on me to-day."

"Mr. Kowalski—"

"Vegas."

"*Vegas.* I'm not here because you've done anything wrong. I wanted to ask you about your tenant upstairs. Alice Hart?"

Vegas shrugged, bringing his eyes back to Kelly. "Saw her yesterday."

Kelly allowed a smirk to cross his lips. "Yeah. My guess is you're not going to see her anymore, Vegas."

"Why?"

"Well, if we go upstairs, I think we're going to find that she's packed up. *Gone.*"

"Really?"

"Do you think we could do that?" Kelly asked, nodding his head toward the door. "Go up to the apartment?"

Vegas shrugged. "Sure. She didn't say she was leaving. I mean, she paid three months in advance. I don't want any trouble."

"She didn't happen to pay in cash, did she, Vegas?" Kelly asked, standing from the booth, encouraging Vincent to join him.

Vegas looked to his feet as he dug the master keys to the apartment from his pocket. "I don't remember."

"Try." Kelly stared down the fry cook, blocking his way from the back of the diner to the front door.

"Yeah, okay. She might've paid in cash. But I always report that income to the IRS, Sergeant

Casey."

Kelly let out a small laugh, stepping out of Vegas's way. "I don't give a damn what you do with your money, Vegas. I'm just looking for some facts."

Vegas showed Kelly out of the diner and to the left. Unlocking the door that led to the staircase, he pointed up and allowed Kelly to take the lead to the apartment. "She paid for three months and asked that I leave her alone. She's a writer you know—just wanted privacy. Truth be told, she said she'd tell my wife about my—well, about my girlfriend—if she caught me snooping around in the apartment when she wasn't here. Said she'd know, too," Vegas said, turning the key to open the door.

He flipped on the light switch. Inside, the apartment was empty. The sheets had been stripped from the bed, the drawers were open—any clothes that had been there were gone. The jar she'd taken down from the top cabinet for roses Kelly bought for her was back in its place—the flowers nowhere to be seen. The trash cans were bare, the countertops wiped clean—it was as if no one had ever been there.

"Damn. You were right," Vegas said. "She's gone."

Kelly walked the perimeter of the small studio.

"When I saw her yesterday, she was leaving with a bag of trash. I thought she was—you know—cleaning up," Vegas said, his voice trailing off.

"Did you notice anything else?" Kelly asked, pushing the fabric curtain back that separated the bathroom from the kitchen. The studio was small, and like most older apartments in New York, all the plumbing was centrally located.

Vegas stared off into his own world. "No."

"Nothing?" Kelly asked as he walked to the bed to look between the mattresses and under the frame.

Vegas shook his head. "She *did* get a package. I delivered it to her."

"What kind of package?"

Vegas didn't look Kelly's way when he shrugged his shoulders, still lost in thought.

"Was it big? Small?" Kelly got in Vegas's face.

"About yea big," Vegas said, showing Kelly

with his hands. "Size of a pencil box. It was just a brown box with her name on it. No address or return address. I thought it was kinda weird."

"What did she say?"

Vegas shrugged his shoulders and made a duck face. "Nothin'. She just took it and left. She was kind of in a hurry now that I think about it."

"I'll bet." Kelly replied, hanging his hands on his hips and walking away.

"If that's it, Sergeant—"

Kelly turned abruptly to face him. "Is there somewhere you need to be, *Vegas*?"

Vincent *Vegas* Kowalski rubbed his hands together and rocked on his feet. "I kind of have an appointment with my lady friend. If I don't keep it, she'll worry and the last thing I need is for her to be calling around looking for me—if you know what I mean."

Kelly took a deep breath. The studio apartment was turning up nothing, although he didn't know what he expected to find there anyway. "Sure. No problem. Do you care if I take a piss before I go?"

"Nah, go ahead," Vegas said, waving him on. "Turn out the lights if you don't mind. The doors will all lock behind you, so just make sure you have everything when you leave, because I'm gone. If you know what I mean."

Kelly nodded. "I'll be in touch if I have any more questions."

"Sure."

Vegas shut the door and Kelly stood in the small studio and shook his head. "What in the hell are you up to?"

Walking to the bathroom, he threw back the fabric curtain that was the only barrier between the bathroom and the rest of the place. The old shower head dripped from the copper pipes above and Kelly listened to the distant echo as he relieved himself. With a flush he turned on the water and looked at himself in the mirror. A single red hair fell from his head, landing in the white porcelain sink. Turning off the water, he threw back the shower curtain, kneeling at the edge of the tub. There it was. One single, solitary, long, light brown hair.

"*Gotcha*," Kelly whispered.

DAY ONE | 2200 HOURS

LOUD VOICES ROUSED Jane from her slumber. After showering, she'd changed into the one clean set of clothes she had in her backpack then laid her wet head down on the musty pillow, unable to fight sleep—or perhaps she didn't care to anymore. The argument was between a man and woman and the louder it got, the faster Jane came to her feet.

Peeling back the thick plastic-backed curtain filled with years of dust, she eyeballed a set of Harley riders standing by their bikes.

"You're a fucking bitch, you know that, Yolanda?" he yelled, slamming his black helmet down on the seat.

"Well you're a *dick*, Bud, and I'm not listening to your shit for one more goddamned day. Do you hear me?" she asked, pointing a finger directly in his travel-worn face. "I'm sick and tired of you *and* your bullshit.

Jane watched as Yolanda stormed off, pulling the keys from the ignition of her Harley and tucking the helmet under her arm.

"Now just a fuckin' minute."

Jane cracked the door to her motel room, watching Bud scurry after her—the keys to his hog twinkling in the moonlight of the clear night as they hung from the ignition like balls on a bull waiting to be castrated. Jane was just the woman to do it.

Quietly shutting the door, she grabbed her backpack, shoving her dirty clothes inside. She did a quick inventory of the room, stuck the room key in the door and shut it behind her.

Climbing aboard Bud's Harley-Davidson Fat Boy, she turned the rabbit's foot keychain in the ignition and kick-started the bike. The engine's classic *potato potato potato* idle began and Jane's heart immediately thrummed harder. Throwing the helmet on, she backed the bike away from the motel parking lot and sped off down Clara Barton Parkway.

Gripping the accelerator like she was mad at it, she changed gears and picked up speed. Officially now a thief, she only hoped Yolanda was right and Bud *was* a dick. She felt better about taking a dick's Fat Boy. In the end, she knew it would be returned without a scratch. She'd even leave a little something in one of the leather saddle bags as a rental fee. But Jane needed wheels and when a golden opportunity presented itself, she took it, and she didn't look back. Jane never looked back.

It wouldn't take long for Bud to realize his Harley was gone and she watched in her rearview mirror, waiting for him to chase her down after hearing his bike pull away.

Jane needed to find a place to hide out, but more than that, she needed to switch the plate on Bud's motorcycle with another. Heading toward the lights, Jane drove toward D.C., where there would be an over-abundance of night-lifers. All she needed was three minutes with her switchblade to change out the plates on a similar bike—preferably another black hog, so at the very least if she was tailed by a cop and called in, she wouldn't come up stolen.

Heading into the West End and Georgetown area, Jane slowed down, looking for a metrosexual guy in mid-life crisis who'd decided to ride his Harley to work and then to a bar afterwards. She wasn't disappointed. Nestled on M street between a couple of swanky eateries was an old school pub. Parked in the alley—nearly illegally—was a black Harley Sportster. Not the same model or even year, but it was close enough.

Jane pulled into the alley, and turned off the loud bike. In the shadows, she flipped the switchblade open and quickly removed the screws from her stolen bike, taking Bud's plate with her to make the swap.

The transition happened surprisingly smoothly, although Jane noticed she was replacing a Delaware plate for a Virginia plate. They were similar but obviously not the same. She only hoped it would take a couple of days for the owner to notice.

Starting the bike again, she backed out of the alley and began to pull away when she caught a glimpse of a man in the window of the restaurant across the street. For a fleeting moment, Jane waited on the bike for him to turn and face the man with whom he was dining. She needed to see his features in their entirety.

A prickly awareness washed over Jane. She

knew the man's face as she knew all the faces of those on *The List*. It was Four. Four, whose last known location was in Pakistan. But there he was as plain as the nose on Jane's face, sitting and eating dinner not ten miles from the Capitol. She couldn't make out the other man he was with. Suddenly, Matt couldn't be a priority. *Could he?*

Jane drove the Harley down the street, looking for a discreet place to park. She wanted to watch him—follow him. A man like Four didn't come into enemy territory—out in the open like this—unless he was taunting the enemy—the United States.

Turning the bike around, Jane watched him climb into a taxi, saying goodbye with an embrace to his friend. Jane slowed the bike and waited down the street, allowing another car to move in between them. The taxi took off and Jane followed at a reasonable distance, always allowing other vehicles to separate them. It was easy to tail someone in a Ford Fiesta that no one noticed—not so much on a loud-ass Harley.

Driving toward Columbia Heights, the cab dropped Four off at the corner of Fourteenth and Columbia near a 7-Eleven. Jane parked the stolen bike in an open parking spot and killed the engine, dismounted, and walked away, still watching his every move.

He walked down the street to a U-shaped apartment unit at Eve's Court. It was one block from the metro and not the usual dive Jane found most of her targets living in—but then again, Four was not a usual target. He was a high ranking, battle-tested member of the caliphate. How he'd made it onto U.S. soil was a mystery to Jane. She looked for a federal tail—a van or delivery truck parked on the street outside Four's location. Surely someone was watching the man. There was nothing.

Without a key or pass, Jane couldn't follow him into the building. Instead, she walked on, hiding in the bushes to get the best angle on his final destination once inside the apartment complex.

"Shit," she mumbled under her breath as he disappeared up the staircase and beyond her line of sight through the glass doors. Jane leaned back against the building, clutching the rabbit's foot keyring in her hand. She couldn't stay in the bushes all night.

Looking up to the apartment building, a light came on inside the unit on the second floor in the west corner of the building. The door of the small balcony opened and Four stepped outside, taking a brief, but full breath. Jane huddled farther back into the bushes.

Cocksuckingmotherfuckingsonofabitch.

Jane didn't know where she would sleep for the night, but she knew where Four would be laying his head.

DAY TWO | ZERO DARK THIRTY

J ANE SAT IN the empty parking lot and called the number on the wooden placard in front of the boarding house hotel on Kenyon Street from her burner phone. It was near enough to keep an eye on Four and close enough to get on the highway to reach Arlington and Matt—although Matt Matthews had become an afterthought.

The woman answering the phone didn't give Jane much confidence she was awake enough to answer any of her questions. "Ahhhh…Jambo Inn."

"I know it's late. I was looking for a room to rent for a week. All cash—all up front."

The voice on the other end brightened. "One fifty per night. Two-hundred-dollar deposit."

"No problem. I need the room *tonight* if possible."

The woman let out a groan and Jane instinctively spoke up. "I'll make it worth your while."

"How?"

"I'll pay you for yesterday *and* today—since it's midnight and I woke you up."

"You nearby?"

"Around the corner."

"I'll give you ten minutes."

"I'll be there."

"Bring your cash…Miss…" she lingered on the word, waiting for Jane to fill in the blank.

"Bell. Catherine." Jane blurted out the words. "Your ad says there's parking."

"Park your car in the back."

"It's a motorcycle."

"*Whatever.*"

The line went dead and Jane hung up, shifting the weight of her backpack. It was heavier than usual because of the police file—the file that weighed on her shoulders and her mind.

It took Jane less than a minute to ride the

motorcycle one block from the abandoned parking lot to the old painted three story home that had been converted into a hotel. In the dark, she could see whomever she'd spoken with on the phone waiting on the front porch—arms crossed—foot impatiently tapping. When the loud Harley turned into the driveway, the woman shook her head in disgust. Jane wasn't making the best first impression.

She killed the engine quickly, rolling the bike to the most secluded parking spot behind the building, not wanting the ass-end of the Harley visible from the street. Jane hurried around to the front of the red building and hustled up the stairs to greet the owner, or manager—she wasn't sure which.

"Sorry to wake you. I was late getting into town."

"Mmmhmm. Get yo' butt inside, *Catherine Bell*. I got an appointment in the morning and I need my beauty rest. Let's get this over with so you and I can both go to bed."

Jane gave her a single nod and followed her in the front door which she locked behind them. "I'm the owner. Claire. There are some things you need to know. It's late and I'm only gonna say them once, so listen good."

Jane said nothing.

"The doors stay locked. If you leave your key behind, you *will* be locked out. Understand?"

"Yes."

"You get two keys. One to your room and one to the front door. Your key don't fit nobody else's room but yours. You see somebody you like staying in the Jambo? You ain't got no business tryin' to get into their room. And your key won't work. Got it?"

"Yes."

"No drugs. If you do drugs, I'll call the cops. No turning tricks. You start havin' sex with anybody but your husband or boyfriend up in this place, I'll call the cops. Got it?"

Jane heard what Claire was saying, but became distracted as she cased the bottom floor of the small bed and breakfast type hotel. What caught her eye wasn't the charming décor, or even the age of the building—both of which were remarkable. What Jane noticed most was the newspaper on the front desk. On the back page was a photograph and an obituary for General James Prescott Collins.

"May I have this newspaper?" Jane asked, ignoring Claire's informational rant.

"Did you hear what I said about having sex up in your room?"

"Yes. No Sex. May I have the paper? Is it today's?"

"Yeah, take the damn paper," she replied.

Jane snagged it from the countertop, folding it under her arm to follow Claire up the stairs to the second floor.

"Don't leave food around. I don't like bugs. And don't leave your kids around. I'm not a babysitter."

"No food. No kids."

"You get two clean towels every day and clean sheets every other day. You want more than that, you have to pay for it. Understand?"

"Yes." Jane watched her unlock room Two and walk in ahead of her, turning on the lamp by the bed.

The yellow glow cast a ghostly light and dark shadows across the room filled with antique furniture. The hardwood floor had an oval braided rug that was worn in the center from years of use. The four poster bed was cherry and was made up with blue sheets and a patchwork quilt. A marble topped nightstand sat next to it with painted floral hurricane lamp with brass finish. Jane thought it looked like someplace a grandmother would sleep—if she'd ever had one.

It smelled of lavender and cedar and the scent calmed Jane, causing one corner of her mouth to turn up in a half-smile. Claire, on the other hand, was *not* smiling.

"Now, if I did the calculations correctly in my head—*and I always do*—you owe me twelve hundred dollars in cash right about now."

Jane parked her backpack on the bed and opened it, digging inside for her roll of money. Taking twelve one hundred dollar bills out, she counted them one by one into Claire's hand and said two words, "thank you."

"Look Catherine Bell, I don't know nothing about you. But if I did, I'd tell you to find a better place to put your money. Someplace more fittin' than that rag-tag bag. There's some pretty bad folks lurking around these parts of the city—around the parts of *any* city for that matter if you know what I mean."

Jane nodded. "I *do* know. And thank you, Claire."

"Lock this door. Bathroom's right through there," she said, pointing past the bed to a small door by the corner closet. "Get your shower early before the hot water runs out. But you didn't hear that from me and I'll deny it if you bring it up again."

Claire shut the door behind her without saying goodbye or goodnight.

Immediately, Jane opened the newspaper and began reading the obituary of General Collins. It was an account of the man's decorated life as a soldier through his time working with the CIA and Maxtronix. "He is survived by his sister and his godson, Christopher Matthew Matthews, III." Jane dropped the newspaper. Matt Matthews would be at Arlington tomorrow morning in a crowd. It would be an easy kill. A direct injection of 100 milligrams of succinylcholine and he'd drop like a pair of panties on prom night. Paralyzed, his breathing would cease. His heart would stop. His brain would die. The funeral being too much for him to bear, she would plant some cocaine on his body from a corner dealer, also lacing the sux injection. Matt Matthews would be labeled a melancholy man unable to control his grief.

Jane bit her lip. *Why Matt?* She needed to log on and do some serious investigating of Matt Matthews. She'd gone looking for him once, only to find his records were sealed—top secret. She stared at his name in the newspaper and thought of her night with him in Atlanta. His sweet smile, his kind eyes. Pulling his scarf from the bottom of her backpack, she inhaled the smell of him—wrapping the shemagh around her neck and shoulders.

The folder she'd stolen from Kelly peeked out of her backpack. She pulled at it, sliding it from its hiding place. Running her hands across the thick, worn brown pressboard, she fingered the rubber band that held it all together and whispered, "What in the hell am I doing?"

Jane dropped the folder onto the bed. She knew she needed to get to a computer. *Now.* She picked up the set of keys to her room and the front door of the hotel. She'd hustled to get to the Jambo on the motorcycle, but Jane always took note of her surroundings, and the one thing she did see was a well-known twenty-four hour print and ship center.

Jane slung her backpack over her shoulder

and left the Jambo not three minutes after arriving. She left nothing behind.

THE EMPTY COPY shop was well lit and had security cameras everywhere. It wasn't the kind of place Jane liked to hang out. Ever.

"I want to use one of the computers please," she said to the pierced and tattooed kid working behind the counter alone.

Struggling with what looked to be deformed hands, he glanced up from his mundane task of three-hole punching and did a double-take, then stared into Jane's eyes. It was the first time Jane felt like anyone had really looked at her since Kelly had taken her to bed. It was then she realized he wasn't a kid—not really.

"Ah…sure." He wrinkled his forehead and gave her a long and interested look—like she had dirt on her face or her clothes were covered in something heinous or foul. He vacillated between a smile and a smirk. It was as if he'd told a joke and only he knew the punch line. "Over here," he said, coming from behind the counter to point at the large Mac with the monstrous screen. "All you have to do is put in a credit card and sign on. You should be good to go from there. Any print outs you make will be charged to the card."

Jane folded her lips into her mouth. "Can I pay cash?"

He shook his head and narrowed his gaze. "No. Sorry."

Jane mumbled under her breath and looked away. She'd already spent too much time in a place with *eyes*. "Shit."

"Let me guess. You don't have a credit card."

Jane stared at the floor. "Thanks anyway," she said walking toward the door.

"Wait."

Jane didn't wait. Jane kept walking, the automatic doors opening as she neared the exit.

"Jane?"

Jane stopped in her tracks, stunned. She didn't turn.

"Jesus, it *is* you. Jane Doe," he said, his voice rising with excitement. "It's *me*. Jack. *Jack Blue*."

Jane hadn't heard his name since she was twelve years old. Still not turning around, a wave of panic and anxiety came over her along with something else—elation. "Jack?"

"Oh God, is it really you? I thought you were dead."

Slowly, Jane faced the boy from foster home number six. The boy whose mother burned his hands on the stove when he was three because he wouldn't stop crying. Jack who loved peanut butter and called the foster kids they lived with the Brady Bunch because the mother's name was Carol.

Jack Blue stared into Jane's face. His eyes glistened with tears. "Fuck it, man. I knew it was you. It's the eyes," he said, pointing to his own with two fingers. "I *knew* it was you."

Jack walked to her, enveloping her into his arms. Jane fought it at first, then gave in, hugging him back. The longer they embraced, the tighter they held onto each other. "Shit. No way," he said, his voice muffled into her grey hoodie.

Jane pulled away, taking him by the scarred hand and into a corner. "I'm not here, Jack. You can never tell anyone that you've seen me."

"I thought you were dead. I read your fucking obit in the Post-Gazette," he said with a smile. "I like the blonde hair by the way. It looks good on you. But you'd look good no matter what."

"Did you hear me, Jack? Are you listening?"

"Yeah, yeah, yeah." His words sounded off in rapid fire. "What are you doing in D.C.?"

Jane shook her head.

"You aren't gonna tell me."

Jane shook her head again.

"You could tell me but then you'd have to kill me," he said with a joking laugh.

Jane gazed into the dark eyes of her old friend. The boy she'd watched sob when his mother, who never wanted him, died of an overdose in a crack house. The boy she watched fight back when he was whipped for sketching a nude from a book—their crazy foster mom using Jesus as a weapon to punish the kids in her care whenever she wanted. Jane had trusted Jack Blue with her life many times before. But this was different. Jane could never take the chance of endangering her dear friend. "I can't let you get messed up in anything—"

"*Illegal?*"

Jane said nothing.

"Tell me what you need."

Jane blinked hard. It had been longer than she could remember since someone voluntarily wanted to help her—no strings—no ulterior motive—just love. "Are you still drawing dicks on everything, Jack?"

He laughed. "Still drawing. Not as much as I'd like. Got a girl and kid at home to look after. You know how it is."

Jane nodded. "Yeah. Look, I need to research some stuff on a computer. *Now*. And I need to get the hell out of here. *Now*. There are cameras everywhere in here."

Jack glanced above them and back to her. "I can wipe the tape. Don't worry about the cameras. The computer is another subject. It won't work without a card." Jack dug into the back hip pocket of his black pants, his wallet attached to a silver chain. "Here. There's not much in the account, but whatever you need is yours."

Jane slid the card from his fingers and hurried to the first computer in the long bank of machines. Shoving it into the slot, it authorized her transaction and brought up a browser window. Fluidly, Jane logged into the

NSA mainframe. The last time she'd logged into the databank, she'd come up empty. Typing in *Matt Matthews* the database began thinking and then unlike the previous search on Matt, Jane hit the mother lode.

Photos of Matt with his arms around Three, cavorting in meetings with some of the highest ranking members of the Islamic State. Jane's eyes widened. She sat back in her chair in disbelief. It was true. In Atlanta he'd had maps of Three's whereabouts—his locations, his phone number. In New York City, she'd found a Maxtronix drone in the garage of Six. An American made drone on the property of known members of the caliphate—where sarin gas was found and a terror attack stopped— where she saw him with her own eyes on the subway in Times Square—the planned target of the attack. But why kill him in Atlanta? Why get rid of him? Was Three finished with him too?

Jane needed to *not* question orders. She needed to *follow* them. Questioning orders was how she got herself into trouble.

Jane pulled the scarf from around her neck and dropped it to the floor. At once she felt nauseous. Logging out, she pulled Jack's credit card from the machine and stood, her legs shaky under her usually steady demeanor.

"Are you okay?" Jack asked. "You look like you've seen a ghost."

Jane dug into her backpack and found a hundred-dollar bill. Wadding it up in her hand, she passed it to Jack, along with his credit card. "Thank you, Jack. Take care of yourself."

She walked past him without saying good-bye. She didn't have any words left.

"Jane?" he called after her, holding up the scarf she'd left behind. "Are you coming back?"

Jack Blue looked at the crumpled one-hundred-dollar bill in his hand. A wave of shock overcame him. "Hey! Thank you!"

DAY TWO | 0900 HOURS

MATT LOOKED OVER the enormous crowd that had gathered at the Memorial Chapel at Joint Base Myer-Henderson Hall, just outside the stone walls that surrounded Arlington National Cemetery. His view from the lectern was overwhelming and humbling. Congressmen, senators and the highest ranking officers of the military had come to pay their respects to the old man. To Matt's beloved *Collie*.

A man without a family, Matt *was* his family—Matt and his grandfather, the first Christopher Matthew Matthews. Collie had never had much use for Chris Matthews, although he maintained a cordial relationship. For business, true, but mostly for Matt III. Collie's elderly sister sat in the front with Matthew's father. Matt stared at the empty seat that was his own, and hoped Collie was there in spirit to witness the outpouring of love for him—the man who'd been a living legend in the military.

Matt had made it through the majority of the eulogy he'd written late into the night, sleeping at his desk as he'd done so often as a kid cramming for an exam. He knew Collie would find it amusing that he had shown up to the funeral a little late and disheveled—his usual entrance. Matt imagined Collie giving him a grimace and then a smile—later he'd get a slap on the back and a smart remark about being late to his own funeral. Today he was late to Collie's.

Throughout the thirty-minute long tribute to the man loved and respected by so many and his only godson, Matt had managed to elicit laughter and tears from the group gathered there. Matt's head buzzed with adrenaline and heartache for the man who was more of a father to him than his own. Now that Collie and his grandfather were both gone, Matt knew—even if he didn't want to admit it—the time had come to take matters into his own hands. It was time to stand on his own two feet and deal with the consequences of whatever life had in store for him. If Collie and his grandfather had taught him anything, it was how to be a man.

"Collie once told me," Matt said, shifting his weight and casually sliding a hand into the pocket of his black suit. He'd loosened up a bit as he inched to the close of the ode to his godfather. "In this life, you're lucky if you have two or five people whom you can truly call a friend. Someone you can share any thought that comes into your head with—good or bad. A person whose company you enjoy whether you are together constantly or separated by time and distance and come together years later and pick up right where you left off. Someone who will affirm the good in you, and forgive you your transgressions. For many in this room, including myself—that person was James Prescott Collins. When we are finished grieving and we are able to put all of this in perspective, we will be able to focus not on the death of such a great soldier and friend, but on his life.

"As many of you know, Douglas MacArthur was Collie's friend—his mentor. MacArthur once spoke of *the soldier* in a famous speech given at West Point. He said, '*His name and fame are the birthright of every American citizen. In his youth and strength, his love and loyalty, he gave all that mortality can give, He needs no eulogy from me, or from any other man. He has written his own history and written it in red on his enemy's breast.'* Today as Collie is laid to rest surrounded by those he led with honor and loved through so many campaigns, he will finally be with the men and women he never stopped praising—he never stopped missing—he always felt responsible for. The men and women who've written their own history in red on their enemy's breast. He will finally tie his own thread into the tightly woven fabric of men and women who've sacrificed their lives for this country."

Matt looked up from his notes and into the faces of so many who admired the man he spoke of. For a fleeting moment, he questioned his own existence—if he died tomorrow, what would he have to show for it? The pit grew in his stomach as he contemplated that very idea and he knew at once that saving his own ass didn't really matter. He needed to do the right thing.

"Collie was a man who showed patience under adversity. Courage under fire. Modesty in victory. A man who knew too many battlefields that stretched from one end of the world to the other. With blood, sweat and tears, General James Prescott Collins knew the filth of war, the stench of foxholes and trenches, the heat, the storms, the jungles, the atrocities of bloodshed. For most of his life he was one of our nation's lifeguards—a gladiator—a protector. There's a saying, *they don't make them like they used to*, and I do believe God broke the mold when he cast General Collins. He was a protector of liberty and freedom—words that are easily thrown around by men who don't always deserve to use them—men like me. Men who, *like me,* live under the blanket of liberty and freedom men such as Collie provided."

Matt cleared his throat, his emotions getting the best of him.

"I asked Collie once what he thought his greatest accomplishment was. I waited for a fierce war battle fought in the pitch of night or story of a near-miss, near death account in a faraway place no one should ever have to be. Collie replied, *'It hasn't happened yet. My greatest accomplishment will be when I make my final roll call. They'll say my name three times, then strike me from the roll. I'll see Saint Peter at the gates of heaven and he'll say, Collie, we've been waiting for you.'"*

"Collie." Matt took a pause to swallow the lump in his throat. He looked to the ceiling and held back the flood of emotion that overwhelmed his soul and cracked his voice "I know today is that day."

OUTSIDE THE CHAPEL the funeral procession began. Collie's flag-draped casket was carried by eight soldiers through the chapel doors to the waiting caisson. The seven horses were the finest in the stables and were followed by two more—one riderless for the warrior who would ride no more. The lush greenery and rolling hills of Arlington were rich with tradition and heavy with ceremony. The pull of despondency was evident in the faces of all who gathered behind the caisson even if the lump in all their throats wasn't.

The procession began the steady march through Arlington. Matt and his father followed the riderless horse, Collie's elderly sister in wheelchair, was pushed alongside them. Behind, trailed the hundreds of others who'd come to say their goodbyes.

Through the winding and wooded sanctuary they walked, passing the thousands of soldiers who'd been laid to rest before Collie—soldiers dating back to the Civil War. The procession lasted for what seemed an eternity, the only sound echoing off the pavement the hollow clop of the horses's hooves and the soft cadence of the military band in the background—Matt stared at the horses, their heads bowed. Even *they* were sad to be there.

When they finally arrived at the section where Collie was to be buried, the procession stopped. His casket was removed from the caisson and carefully carried to the grave. Matt caught a glimpse of his father taking a full and deep breath and shook his head. Christopher Matthews was a man who didn't care if his son was put to death for treason, just as long as it didn't come back to bite *him* in the ass, why would he care if Collie—the one man who loved his son—was dead and gone?

All the uniformed men and women held their salutes as Collie's casket was carried to the open grave.

Matt and his father sat in the chairs at the edge of the gravesite. Several of the people who'd worked for Collie for years took seats behind them and Matt held onto the fragile hand of Collie's sister. The weather in Arlington was a balmy seventy-five degrees, but her frail and bony fingers were ice-cold. Matt kissed her hand and tried to warm it up in his own before inhaling the sunshine of the day. Even Mother Nature knew better than to mess with Collie's final day in charge.

The Chaplin said a prayer—a muddled mix of words Matt could no longer listen to or decipher. His grief had taken hold of him in the final moments—the sight of the open grave weighing on his heart. Matt and the others rose to their feet when asked to do so by the officer in charge for the presentation of military honors. A thirteen-canon salute boomed throughout the cemetery before the firing party initiated their rifle volleys. Finally, Taps played in the distance and a strong breeze blew through the crowd gathered at the gravesite. It was as if Collie himself was giving a final farewell while the mournful bugle cried along with the hundreds of mourners shedding their own tears.

In perfect form, Collie's casket team removed the flag and began folding it until it was in the shape of the white-starred triangle Matt had seen too many times given to families of the men and women he'd known in the Middle East. Passed to the Old Guard's commander, it then went to the Army's Chief of Staff. Kneeling at the foot of Collie's elderly sister, he pressed the flag into her trembling hands while whispering words of comfort, then moved on to Matt.

Matt didn't listen to what he was saying, it didn't matter anymore. He paid attention to Eloise, Collie's sister, who was tugging at the sleeve of his suit jacket.

"Here, honey." Her voice shook with age and emotion. "I think we both know he would've wanted you to have this. You were his pride and joy."

Matt swallowed hard. Every tear, every feeling he'd kept at bay since learning of Collie's death surfaced like a sunken ship pulled from the depths of the ocean—messy and full of years of shit no one had ever seen. Stepping away from everyone at the gravesite, Matt walked to Collie, the flag held tightly against his chest. Splaying his hand across the top of the mahogany casket, Matt leaned in and whispered. "I won't let you down. I promise."

DAY TWO | 1000 HOURS

KELLY CASEY WALKED the hallway of the NYPD Counterterrorism Bureau. "Chuck!" he shouted over the crowded room, pointing to a balding man who looked as if he hadn't slept in a week.

"Jesus H., Casey! Don't you know *not* to fucking shout at me when I have a hot cup of joe in my hand?"

Kelly always thought of Chuck Jordan as the kind of nervous little shit who would get himself or someone else killed in the line of duty, but behind the desk he was a master. "What the hell. It's already ten. Shouldn't you be on cup number sixteen by now?" Kelly asked with a wicked smile.

Known not only for his abilities to track terrorists from behind his computer, Chuck was also famous for being a caffeine addict. Kelly always figured it would be the death of the guy. They'd find him in his cubicle, dead from a stroke with a Twinkie in one hand and a cold cup of shitty precinct coffee in the other.

"Shut the fuck up. You never come back here and show you're pretty little ginger face unless you need something, so give."

Kelly made his way to Chuck's cubicle, taking a stack of files from the only chair next to the desk and placing them in his lap as he sat. Chuck bristled at the mere movement of anything that belonged to him. Kelly watched him silently fidget in his seat and stare. "What the hell do you want, anyway, Casey?"

Kelly smiled. "Now don't be that way."

"Just give me the case number so I can add whatever I'm about to do to the file."

Kelly leaned in, gripping the folders in his lap. "There's no file for this."

"Then what the hell? You know I don't have time for stupid shit." Chuck drained the last gulp of coffee from his cup and stacked it on the desk inside the dozen other empty Styrofoam cups.

"I need to find a woman."

Chuck looked at his computer and continued working. "Don't we all," he mumbled.

"I thought you were dating the chick from payroll."

Chuck shook his head back and forth, but didn't look at Kelly.

"Didn't work out, huh?"

Again Chuck shook his head.

"Wanna talk about it?"

Chuck went into shutdown mode. It was obvious he was done with Kelly Casey and his questions. Still, Kelly sat in the chair and watched—waited. Finally ceasing his incessant typing, Chuck stared at his monitor and spoke. "What do I have to do to get you the fuck out of my cubicle? Just tell me and I'll do it."

"I need to look through video footage at Penn Station. Someone I was…"

"Tracking?"

"Kinda."

"Stalking?"

"*No*," Kelly replied, dragging out the word. "She knows something about this last case—the one in Queens."

"Oh," Chuck brought his voice down. "The sarin gas?"

Kelly nodded. It was clear he needed

Chuck's help, but he didn't want to say much about it, nor did he want it associated with the active case.

"Who we looking for?"

Kelly shook his head. "She's using an alias. I'm sure of it. I've got a DNA sample and I'm running it through, but we both know how long that could take."

Chuck let out a laugh, then shoved a potato chip in his mouth and began to speak as he chewed. "So you don't have a name. Got a photo? Something I can use for facial recognition?"

Kelly shook his head.

"Then what in the actual fuck do you even want? You wanna sit and look through hours of footage with the hope of finding her?"

"Look," Kelly said. "I know where she's gonna end up—eventually. I just need to know where she is *now*. Where she went when she left here. That's all. And if I need to look through a few hours of tape, I will. If I don't find anything then so be it—but at least I will have looked."

"Do you even know *when* she might have left town?"

"I'm taking a wild guess, but yesterday. Probably early in the morning, but possibly the night before."

Chuck shook his head. "Where do you want to start? I'll get you set up on a monitor over there," he said, pointing to an empty corner over his shoulder without looking. "You can watch until your little heart's desire. But I gotta tell you. If you don't know who or what you're looking for, it's a needle in a haystack."

Kelly nodded. "I understand."

Chuck started working his computer magic and stopped only to eat another chip.

"What can I do to help?" Kelly asked.

Chuck handed Kelly the stack of empty Styrofoam cups from his desk without looking at him. "Get me another cup of coffee. And you might want to get one for yourself. You're gonna be here for a while."

DAY TWO | 1030 HOURS

FROM THE EDGE of the woods she watched him. Dressed in black pants, shirt and dark sunglasses, Jane blended into the crowd of mourners at General Collins' funeral like a grain of sand on the beach. The crowd was unmanageable by Arlington security. Jane had worked her way in by pinching a White House employee badge then talking and smiling her way past any security measure that wanted to stop or question her.

Truth be told, she was touched by the eulogy Matt had given in the chapel. She'd stayed outside and well away from his line of sight, but had heard his heartfelt tribute all the same. Now that the graveside service had concluded, people were starting to scatter. Jane held back, keeping an eye on Matt Matthews, who stood at the edge of the burial plot.

Jane replayed every moment she'd spent with him—every conversation—every kiss—every touch. She considered herself an impeccable judge of character and Matt Matthews didn't give off *that* vibe to her—the one that put her senses on alert and told her to steer clear, to stay away. To kill him. And yet here she was, watching her kill assignment—casing him to best decide how to end his life. How would she end the life of the man she'd fantasized running away with? She watched him sink his head into his chest. He was clearly undone by the death of his friend and mentor. A mentor who didn't know his own godson was aiding and abetting the Islamic State.

Jane couldn't take it. She simply couldn't watch any longer. Matt Matthews was low hanging fruit. She could take him out at any moment. This *wasn't* the moment. She turned and began to blend into the crowd—a crowd that somehow began to bottleneck. Blocked by armed guards, there was only one way out of Arlington on foot and now that the funeral was over, security was tightening up and forcing everyone to leave through a single exit.

Jane did everything she could to find an

alternative route, including turning back toward the gravesite to exit the opposite direction of the masses. Like a salmon swimming upstream, she turned again and decided to wait out the crowd by an enormous oak tree, turning her back to gaze upon the endless rows of headstones.

A cool breeze blew through the cemetery and Jane took off her sunglasses to run her frustrated hands through her blonde hair. Taking a deep breath, she watched as the dissipating crowd brushed past her. She decided if she waited one minute longer, security would loosen as the crowd moved toward the exit and she could work her way out of Arlington the way she came in—through the back.

Jane ticked off the seconds in her head as she counted the people. One by one they walked with the crowd, hugging and chatting about the day—the eulogy—the great man that General Collins was. Then she felt it. A tap on her right shoulder.

She didn't turn. She began walking away.

"Wait."

She felt a hand on her arm, spinning her around. She had two choices: she could let it happen or she could break the arm attached to the hand. She let it happen.

She turned. Matt Matthews stared her in the face.

"I knew it was you."

Jane said nothing.

"I'd know your—*your*—I'd know you from behind anywhere. What are you doing here?"

She stared at him, blinking.

"You've changed your hair. You're…you're *blonde.*"

Still Jane said nothing.

Matt Matthews wrapped his arms around her, pulling her in tight. Jane could feel him breathing on her neck in between light kisses to her cheek and lower jaw. Still she remained silent, but managed to place her hands on his back.

"This whole day has been shitty—the worst. And then I saw you and I thought," he whispered in her ear. "I don't know what I thought. I just—just seeing you again makes it better somehow."

Pulling away, Jane looked to their feet. She was at a loss.

"Hey," Matt said, lifting her chin with a

single finger. He stroked her cheek, brushing a stray hair from her eyes. Jane felt herself go numb.

And then he did it. Matt Matthews leaned in without warning and kissed her. First it was a simple peck, but he came back and kissed her hard. Obviously fueled by uncertainty and raw emotion, Matt Matthews let go—and all over Jane.

Jane could feel the kiss go deep into her body—it was the kiss she'd dreamed about on the pink shores of a distant beach. It was the smell of his scarf—the smell of Matt Matthews. It was the scent of the man she'd been sent to kill.

"MATTHEW!" SOMEONE CALLED from behind them in the crowd.

Matt pulled his lips from hers, a smile plastered across his face. "Hold that thought," he said, letting her go and turning to answer to his name.

Christopher Matthews called out to him. "Matthew, we're meeting the limousine behind the chapel."

Matt nodded and pointed in the general direction his father needed to walk, then turned back to question the beautiful woman he'd just kissed.

She'd vanished.

"Hey!" he shouted as he frantically began to look for her. "Scar—" Matt stopped in his tracks. It was no use. She was gone. Matt shook his head and stopped to lean his body against the huge oak tree where he'd found her. Closing his eyes, he placed his hands on his head, rubbing his face in frustration.

"Don't turn around." The voice was deep, male and undistinguishable.

"What?"

"Don't. Turn. Around."

"Who are—"

"Listen to me and don't make a sound. She's been sent to kill you. Get out now. Leave town. I can't help you again."

"What?" Matt asked, dropping his fisted hands to his sides in muted irritation.

The voice didn't answer. Matt turned on a dime to find the space behind him once again empty. "What the fuck?"

DAY TWO | 1200 HOURS

KELLY CASEY HAD spent the past two hours poring over what seemed to be eons of footage. In his hand he held two things: the only piece of the police report she didn't steal from his safe—a marked map of Pittsburgh, and the latest intel briefing on Siad al Daleel ul Khyayraat. He was on the move and in Washington, D.C. Kelly Casey didn't work for the FBI, and he wasn't CIA, but he knew if the woman he was tracking—the woman who'd stolen his father's police report and killed Al-Sistani in Queens had even remotely studied the nearly thirty-year-old report, she was hot on a trail and either on her way, or already in D.C. He just needed to confirm it before taking off on a wild goose chase. Kelly knew if he could locate Siad—he'd find her close by.

Chuck closed in on Kelly like a cat quietly

observing or perhaps silently judging. Kelly spoke to him without turning his head. "I don't like you reading over my shoulder, Chuckie. What is it?" Kelly heard the rustling of plastic and knew Chuck was helping himself to more sugar. Whether it was another Twinkie or a bag of Cheez Doodles it was hard to tell.

"You're doing it wrong," Chuck mumbled through a half-masticated Ding Dong.

Kelly swiveled in his chair to face him and grimaced—mostly at the food falling from Chuck's mouth. "What in the hell are you talking about?"

"You're focusing on the whole damn station. You gotta focus on the doors, man. *The doors.*"

Kelly turned his palms up and shook his head. "What the fuck, Chuck?"

"Yeah," he replied, his mouth finally vacant of chocolate mush. "I get that question a lot. Get out of the chair. I'll show you what I mean."

Kelly relinquished his position in front of the three monitors set side by side in a semi-circle on the table. "See?" Chuck said, tapping away, bringing up a side window of background code. "When you zoom in on only the doors of the train, you can see who is getting on and off."

In rapid-fire succession, the tape sped up and slowed down as each of the trains at Penn Station bound for Washington D.C. stopped and slowed for the arrival and loading and unloading of the train—every time zooming in on each of the entrances via separate camera angles.

"Why in the hell have I been sifting through this shit all morning like a slug, Chuck?"

Chuck shrugged his shoulders and dug food out of his teeth with his tongue, making an odd face—a face Kelly wanted to punch. "Job security, dude. If I showed anybody how to *really* work all this crap, who would need me?"

Kelly shook his head. "I swear to God if I didn't have a soft spot for you, I'd knock your ass into next Thursday, you little shit."

Chuck smiled, then took a huge bite of his Ding Dong, and started talking with his mouth open all over again. "But you won't. Because you need me."

Kelly looked away, glancing at the center monitor. A hooded woman caught his eye. "Stop! Stop it right there."

Chuck turned in the seat and tapped on the keyboard, stopping the black and white footage. "Back that up," Kelly commanded.

Chuck backed up the tape and restarted the footage. A woman in a zip-up hoodie walked into view and paused just before getting onto the D.C. bound train. She looked suspiciously to the man on her left, giving the camera a decent view of her shadowed features. A flash of light came from somewhere and she ducked onto the train.

Kelly leaned into the monitor closer. "*Sonofabitch*. Back it up again and go frame by frame."

"You got it, boss."

Again, the woman walked to the door of the train—jeans and a grey zip-up hoodie pulled over her head. The frames inched along as she turned her head toward the man next to her. He pulled his phone from his pocket and turned it on. The light from his phone illuminated her face for a split-second. "There." Kelly said. "Can you enhance that?"

"Of course."

Chuck zoomed in. The image was grainy, but right in front of Kelly Casey's eyes was the woman with whom he'd had an amazing night of lovemaking. The woman who'd taken his keys and stolen his father's file. The woman Kelly *knew*, whether he could prove it or not, was responsible for killing Al-Sistani. "*Gotcha.*"

"She took the Acela Express to—"

"Union Station, Washington, D.C.," Kelly said, staring at the blinking image on the screen.

"Departed oh-six-hundred-hours yesterday morning," Chuck reported. "She's got a lead on you, dude."

"Yeah," Kelly murmured. "But I know exactly who she's going to see."

Kelly's cellphone rang out in his pocket as Chuck stood and patted him on the back. "Want an eight by ten glossy to commemorate the occasion?" he asked.

Kelly nodded and answered his phone. "Casey."

"Sergeant Casey, this is Dr. Randall Emerson with the FBI."

"Yeah?" Kelly had a hard time hiding the surprise in his voice.

"I had a request come through from your counterterrorism field office for a DNA match."

Kelly knitted his brow and hung his hand on his hip. He didn't expect a result back anytime soon, but what he really didn't expect was a call from the FBI. "Yes, Dr. Emerson. I did make a DNA match request, but honestly I figured it was a dead end and I didn't think I'd hear from anyone, let alone so soon."

"Yeah. Well."

Kelly waited for the agent to continue but the conversation was nothing but silence—each waiting for the other to continue. Finally, Kelly spoke. "Dr. Emerson, *you* called me."

More silence.

"Was there a match? Doctor?"

"Look. I'm not supposed to tell you this and I don't really know why I am, other than the fact that personally I don't think it matters. Someone above me seems to think it does."

"Go on," Kelly said.

"The DNA is a match to a Marine. Corporal Jane Doe, legally deceased. Declared Missing in Action, Baghdad, Iraq, June 2014. It seems as though she's in the database from a child abandonment case. I can only surmise it's the reason her name is Jane Doe. I mean, that's really something. Right?"

Kelly's breath hitched. He couldn't find the ability to form a single word to respond. Deep in his heart—in his subconscious mind, he *knew* it was her, but the confirmation made it all too real.

"Hello? Sergeant Casey?"

"Yeah," Kelly murmured, his mouth too dry to articulate much more. "I'm still here. Thanks for the call. And ah…" he paused to clear his throat and find his voice. "Don't worry, Doc. Now that I know the sample is old—well, you know—I appreciate you filling me in. Even if you were told not to."

"Yeah, like I said. I don't see what the big deal is. I mean, the woman is long gone now. So—"

Kelly paused, thinking of all the nights his father stayed up late, focusing on Jane's file— wondering who was so hell-bent on keeping her case hidden. "Dr. Emerson," Kelly blurted at the last second. "Just out of curiosity, what *were* you supposed to tell me?"

After a long pause, he answered. "I was

politely told to lose the sample."

Kelly leaned forward in his chair, feeling his father's presence and frustration around him like a heavy coat. "Thanks, Doc," Kelly mumbled, his face now buried inside his own hands.

Kelly ended the call and stood to pace, sliding his phone into the back pocket of his dark jeans.

"Who was that?" Chuck asked, handing him a photo-capture of Jane boarding the train. Kelly stopped and stared at the enlarged photograph, at the image of the one person his father searched for his entire career. He blinked through a hooded gaze. It was almost poetic that Jane had stumbled into his life. Now he had no choice but to find her. Because sooner or later, *he* would be coming after her.

"Casey?"

Kelly ignored Chuck. Pulling his phone from his back pocket, he dialed. The phone rang twice before she picked up. "Whadduwant, motherfucker?"

"Nice way to answer your phone, Mary Charles."

"Damn you, Casey."

"Sorry. Nice way to answer your phone, *Charlie*." Kelly mouthed the words, *thank you* to Chuck, shook his hand, then brushed the leftover crumbs from Chuck's fingers off on his pant leg and blew out of the double doors of the office.

"Again I say, what do you want, shithead?" Charlie blurted out the question and Kelly was quickly reminded of her lack of decorum.

Mary Charles *Charlie* Madewell was one of the toughest officers Kelly Casey had ever had the privilege of working alongside. Smart, funny, and more knowledgeable than most of her male counterparts, she was one of the best in the business when it came to counterterrorism. She'd trained in New York alongside Kelly, but left the city behind, opting for Washington, D.C. and the Secret Service when the opportunity arrived. They'd always remained friends and they'd only been lovers once—on a cold and drunken night after they'd both barely escaped death. It was more of a friendly celebration of *we made it out alive*—a roll in the hay—not a hot, sexy or meaningful encounter. After, Kelly never forgot Charlie's words as she slipped her panties back on. *Well, that was a big fucking mistake.*

They both regretted it and vowed to never speak of it again. They also confessed they weren't the least bit attracted to the other and wanted to instead remain friends—name-calling friends—but friends all the same.

"Settle down, fuck face," Kelly replied, dishing out his own barb. "You know I only call you when I need a favor."

"It better not be sexual," Charlie quipped.

Kelly couldn't help but smile at the sound of her voice. Charlie was a true friend. Kelly trusted her with his life and he knew she felt the same about him. "Jesus. I'm not *that* hard up."

"From what I can remember, you're not that hard."

"Nice."

"Out with it, fire-crotch. What's on your mind?"

"Wondering if you have a twenty on our old friend, Siad."

Charlie went silent.

"Charlie?" Kelly asked, climbing into his car to start the engine. He needed to drive to his apartment, pack up a few clothes, a couple of extra guns and some ammo before leaving town. "Charlie, did I lose you?"

"No."

"What?"

Charlie lowered her voice. "What are you up to?"

"Nothing," Kelly replied in his most convincing tone.

"Fuck you, Casey. Tell me the truth."

Kelly leaned into the window of the car and rubbed his eyes. He wasn't frustrated with Charlie, but tired. Tired of playing games. Tired of being in the dark. He needed answers. Straight forward and truthful answers. "I'm curious if he's in your neck of the woods. Is there any chatter? Are you keeping an eye on him?"

"What do you think?"

Kelly let out a little laugh. "You know I know you're watching him like a hawk so just tell me what's going on, Charlie. I'd do it for you."

"He rolled into town yesterday. We've got surveillance on him."

"And?"

"That's it, dude. You know the drill. We can only watch the asshole."

Kelly turned into the long loop that surrounded the buildings of his apartment complex. "Look, I'm coming into town. Think you can put me up for a couple of nights?"

Charlie let out a heavy sigh on the other end of the line.

"Hello?"

"My girlfriend might take issue with your ginger-junk hanging around the apartment."

Kelly blanched and his jaw tightened as he put his car in park and turned off the ignition. "Wait. What?"

"I'm serious, Kelly."

"You have a—"

"I didn't stutter, motherfucker. I have a girlfriend."

"Hey," Kelly shifted his tone from their usual acerbic banter and softened his voice. "I actually think that's great, Charlie. Really. I'm serious. I'm happy for you. I mean, if you're happy."

"I'm happy."

"I can check into a hotel somewhere. It's no big deal. I don't want to put you out."

"Now you really *are* being a little bitch. If you're coming to D.C., you're staying with me," Charlie replied. "Besides, who's gonna keep your pansy-ass out of trouble? God knows you can't do it on your own."

"Seriously, Charlie. I need a twenty on him. Last known location."

Kelly could hear her working over her keyboard rapidly. She always did treat her computer like it was her bitch, pounding the keys like they needed the punishment. "I don't know about this, Kelly."

"Just give it to me, Charlie."

"Eve's Court. It's an apartment complex at the corner of Columbia and Fourteenth Streets in Columbia Heights."

Kelly scribbled the information down on the back of a scrap piece of paper in his car. "Got it."

"And Kelly?"

"Yeah?"

"You didn't get that from me. And one more thing."

"What?" Kelly asked, shutting the door to his car and locking it with the fob as he rushed into his building to pack up.

"Don't do anything stupid. At least, not without me."

"You got it."

DAY TWO | 1500 HOURS

O UT OF HIS suit and into his usual rumpled button down and khakis, Matt walked about the gardens at his father's estate in Potomac. Hands clasped behind his back, he paced, thinking of his past, thinking of Collie, thinking of what was ahead for him. Through the fountain that separated the rose garden from the west end of the Matthews mansion, Matt could see his father milling about through the French doors that led into his study. His father was always pacing—always dictating. He never typed anything. He never could. When texting and email became all the rage years ago, Matt's father was quick to have voice to text software developed for that very purpose. It wasn't widely known, but Maxtronix was the pioneer of speech recognition software thirty years ago, selling the technology to the computer industry, taking the talk-to-text industry global. Little did they all know it started because one very powerful man didn't know, or simply refused to learn, how to use a qwerty keyboard.

Matt watched his father through the window like a hawk—his senses still on high alert, his body emotionally drained from the day. Matt struggled with what to do next. Collie was dead. He'd called in to come out of the field, but was told to wait for further instructions. Further instructions for *what*, he had no idea. Matt was done. Finished. He'd done his time. He'd given the U.S. government everything they'd asked for. He'd infiltrated the caliphate—he'd buddied up with the worst of the worst. He'd traded his soul for secrets and what he'd discovered was that his dad was a traitor. Now that he wanted out, he was in deeper than he could've ever imagined—all because his father was greedy. Collie always said, *pigs get fat. Hogs get slaughtered.* Matt was being led to the slaughter house. And by his own father.

"Matt, get in here!"

Christopher Matthews yelled from the open door of his study onto the perfectly manicured lawn of the estate. Waving his arm into his body he shouted twice at his son and made a face. "Do you hear me?"

Shoving his hands in his pockets, Matt tucked his bottom lip into his mouth and slowly began putting one foot in front of the other, making his way down the path to his father. The aviator sunglasses he wore covered the disgust in his eyes, but couldn't conceal the smirk on his face. Matt Matthews could barely stand to be near his father, let alone follow his orders.

When he finally stepped foot across the threshold and into his father's study he simply stared at him, not taking off the sunglasses.

Christopher did a double take upon seeing him and twisted his face in disapproval. "What are you doing? Take off those damn sunglasses."

Disdain seeped from every pore of Matt's rigid body. It was all he could do to keep from throwing one lights-out, devastating punch to his father's face. He nearly shook with hatred and adrenaline. Still, he said nothing.

"We need to go over some business," Christopher said taking a seat behind his desk.

Matt remained standing near the French doors as if ready to make a clean getaway at any moment. A sour look overcame Christopher's tan and deep-set wrinkled face. "What the hell are you doing? Come sit down."

He chastised Matt as if he was a boy. It fueled Matt's hate-fire for his father all the more. "What is it, Dad? I have some things I need to do."

His father scoffed. "Like what?"

Matt calmed his urge to put a fist through the wall, or his father's nose. "I wanted to go to the office—make a good start tomorrow."

Christopher looked him up and down. His facial expression was one of disbelief, but he shrugged anyway. "Okay. But first we talk some business *here*. I need you to sign some papers."

Turning a file folder around, Matt's father pushed a stack of legal documents with small Post-it note tabs attached to the empty lines where Matt's full and legal name resided underneath.

Matt stared at the one-inch stack of papers. "What's all this?"

His father walked away, flipping a nonchalant hand in his direction. "If you're taking on more responsibility at Maxtronix, I want you to make some money. These documents give you more power and a salary instead of your usual allowance." Christopher finally turned to face him. "All you need to do is sign."

Matt took a deep breath, pulling the stack from the desk and onto his lap. His father walked to him, placing a heavy hand on his shoulder before slipping a pen from his jacket pocket and into Matt's fingers.

"Dad, I'm not going to sign them *right now*. I'll look everything over and get them back to you."

"What do you mean, you aren't going to sign them?"

Matt stood, folding the top page over and closing the file folder. "Just what I said. I'm not signing. Not now. It's been a long day. We just buried Collie, for God's sake. Can't I take a moment to decompress? What the hell is wrong with you anyway?"

Christopher Matthews paced the floor of his dark, although beautifully decorated study. Emblematic of the rest of the house, it looked more like a room in a museum than a working office. Nothing in the Matthews' mansion looked as though it had ever been touched, nor should it be. A somber and cold place, it was indicative of the man himself. "Nothing is wrong with me, Matthew. This is *business* and if you're going to be in business with *me*, then you damn well better learn how to conduct it because this is how it works. The world doesn't care if your feelings are hurt. Business doesn't stop because you have a fucking runny nose. Do you understand? This isn't *writing*. This isn't *journalism*. This is the real world where we do real fucking business. If I fail, there are hundreds of thousands of people whom I employ who fail too. *Do you understand?*" Matt watched his father's face turn red as his voice rose. "If this company goes south, all those people whom I employ, I provide health insurance for, whose salaries I pay which in turn sends their children to private school and college, pays for dance lessons and football uniforms—all of that goes away for them if I'm not holding up my end of the deal. *Do. You. Understand?*"

Matt stepped away from his father, now nearly foaming at the mouth, and nodded.

"Then just sign the fucking papers!" Christopher's face was beet red. He turned and walked back to his chair and sat, slowly wiping his hand against his hairline.

Calmly, Matt stepped toward the door that led into the long hallway and away from his father's study. Tucking the file folder under his arm, he paused at the threshold. Turning, he faced his father. "I know what you're doing."

Christopher shook his head in disgust, his voice now calm, quiet. "What are you talking about?"

Matthew drew his finger and with the steely gaze of his grandfather before him, looked through Christopher Matthews and pointed with each word proclaiming his one victory. "*I. Know.*"

DAY TWO | 1700 HOURS

MATT TOOK THE elevator to his new office at Max HQ. Before he'd even sat in the worn leather chair of his grandfather, he called Peter.

"Meet me."

Matt met him at the stairwell where he followed Peter down the stairs and into the secret section of Max HQ. Through the pressurized doors and past the facial recognition biometric, the retinal scan and the vein authentication key they progressed. Neither said a word until they'd made it into the lab. "We'll set you up with complete clearance tomorrow," Peter said. "I want you to be able to come and go from here without me."

Matt nodded. "I got in a fight with Dad."

"Too much funeral?" Peter asked.

"Too much Dad."

Matt tossed the legal folder on the lab countertop, opening the file. "He wants me to sign these. I haven't looked through them, but I can only imagine what they are. Any way we can have a legit attorney eyeball them from *my* point of view and make changes?"

Peter narrowed his steely gaze. "You ready to dance with the devil like that?"

Matt blinked deliberately. "Yes."

"I'll take care of it," Peter said, closing the folder and tucking it under the wing of his white lab coat. "I'm glad you're here. I've got some things to show you."

"Are these good things or bad things? Because after putting Collie in the ground and literally wanting to punch the smug look off my father's face this afternoon, I don't know how much more I can handle."

"Trust me," Peter said with a crooked smile. "You're gonna want to see this. Follow me."

Matt followed Peter through two more sets of double doors. The labs, usually brightly lit, had become dark. A soft ray emitted light from under an extra soffit that surrounded the perimeter of the room. In the center of the black floor was a small red circle six inches in diameter. The entire space looked like something from a futuristic pod. "Where are we?"

"Welcome to the testing facility of the Maxtronix Division of Micro Insect Air Vehicles. Or as we like to call them, Mia V's."

"What?" Matt's voice was breathy with shock.

"Bugbots. Nanodrones. We began developing them before your Gran passed."

"Are you kidding me right now? This is the stuff the Air Force has been dicking around with for years."

"Still are. But we've perfected it. Nothing like private money from war profiteering to fuel research and development. It's amazing what can happen when there's not a congressional oversight committee always looking over your shoulder."

"So?" Matt shrugged in excited anticipation.

"So what?"

"Show me."

"You're in the room with five of them right now."

Matt's eyes widened and a smile crept across his face. "No way."

Peter nodded. "Hold your right arm out in front of you. Palm facing down."

Matt did as he was told.

"Be very still," Peter said, donning a set of amber lab glasses before placing a pair over Matt's eyes as well.

"Lights," Peter whispered. The faint lighting dimmed even more upon his command.

"How will I see it Peter?"

"Your glasses detect ultraviolet light. You'll see her."

"Her?"

"Yes. *Her.*"

Matt stood perfectly still. The quiet of the room was unnerving as he waited patiently for *her* to show herself. "Peter I—" And there she was. The tiniest of green dots, it was indeed an insect. With six legs, a head, two antennae, a thorax, abdomen, two elongated wings and a proboscis for sucking blood. "It's a mosquito."

"No. But she sure looks and acts like one."

Matt took his eyes off the bug to glance at Peter. He stood satisfied with his arms crossed. On his face was the type of smirk only a scientist who'd struck gold could have.

"What's she capable of?"

"Death, my friend. She's lethal."

The nanodrone flew away and Matt dropped his arm back to his side. "What do you mean *lethal?*"

"Mia V's are armed with tetrodotoxin. It's twelve hundred times deadlier than cyanide. A lethal does is smaller than the head of a pin, so we quadruple it and paralyze the victim on the spot. They become essentially a human zombie. Then they die."

"Tetrodotoxin? Puffer fish?"

Peter grinned from ear to ear, obviously pleased with himself and nodded. "You got it."

"And there are five of them in the room with us right now?"

Peter looked above and around the two of them as they stood in the center of the room. "All you have to do is look for them—but look hard. In the light of day, no one will ever see one coming. It's the latest technology in clandestine weaponry."

"You can say that again."

"You can also see why your father has never been made aware of what goes on in this lab."

Matt nodded somberly. Even *with* Mia V, there was still the problem of his father. There was still the problem of fifty-two drones in the hands of the Islamic State. "This is cool and everything Peter, but how is it going to help us take out those drones? I can't get ahead of myself. I'm going to be tried for treason if someone doesn't kill me first."

"Kill you?" Peter asked, taking off his glasses. "Lights."

The lights came up and Matt took off his glasses as well. "Today at Arlington. After everything was over, I saw someone—someone I met a couple of weeks ago. She's...I dunno...she's someone special, and I mean that in more than one way. I walked over to talk to her. Dad called out to me and I took my eyes off of her for only a moment—then she was gone. Then a man with a deep voice grabbed my shoulder from behind and told me *not* to turn around. The only thing he said to me was, *she's been sent to kill you.*"

"*Who* was sent to kill you? The woman? The someone … *special?*" Peter asked, crossing his arms in front of his chest.

Matt shook his head and stared at the floor. "I don't know. Maybe. I've seen her in action. She's fully capable. I think she's covert ops of some kind, but who knows. She disappeared on me in Atlanta and she disappeared on me again today."

"I don't know what to say to you, Matt. I'll help you in any way I can. These micro drones are at your disposal. *I* am at your disposal. Tell me what you want to do and I'll do it."

Matt looked at Peter. For the first time in as long as he could remember, he felt like he had someone he could trust other than Collie. With the old man gone, it was nice to have an ally. He was going to need it.

"I wish I knew what I needed Peter. I'd be happy to give some orders. I just don't know. I mean, what *exactly* do we need to—?"

"We need those codes to activate the suicide assignment and self-destruct element. One set of numbers is preset here, the other is computer generated and randomly assigned. We need them both to activate the sequence."

"And you said Maxtronix doesn't have a record for these?"

Peter shook his head. "As far as our records are concerned, technically these drones don't exist."

"Then how would Dad have gotten the information to whomever he traded the drones to for the oil? The numbers had to go out somehow."

Peter nodded. "Indeed."

Matt began to pace the perimeter of the room and think aloud. "He wouldn't use the phone—the other end might not be secure. What line of communication would he have that he could send out numbers and make it look like it was nothing in particular when it was something so specific like codes?"

"Numbers could be anything," Peter replied.

"Yeah, but it's not so much what the numbers are—at least not at first. First we need to know where his emails are going. Is there any way we could see his emails to the Middle East within the timeframe we know the drones went out? At least start there?"

Peter nodded. "Sure, but your father's been taught to clear his hard drive. We all use disk space cleaners and optimizers. If he's deleted his emails, they're gone. The info is shredded virtually and the hard drive wiped of the information. There's no data remanence."

"*Really?* He knows how to do that? I mean the man is virtually helpless. I watched him through the door today in his office. He can't even type. He dictates everythi—" Matt stopped cold in his tracks. "Peter."

Peter looked to him but didn't say a word.

"What does Ava record?"

"The Automated Voice Activated software?"

Slowly, Matt nodded his head. "Ava was in the New York Penthouse. She's in the office and at my father's home in Potomac."

"She's in Aspen and Tuscany," Peter confirmed. "And she records *everything.*"

"Can you hack into that system and retrieve everything my father's said to her?"

"I *wrote* that system."

A slow and satisfying smile curled across Matt's lips.

"Peter, get those codes."

DAY TWO | 2100 HOURS

JANE STOOD AT the edge of the wooded area that was the Maxtronix campus. She'd followed Matt Matthews from his father's estate on the Potomac River, keeping her distance on the Harley. She needed to finish the assignment and quickly. She wanted to move on to finding Three, and then on to Pittsburgh where she'd have time to sort through her own life—her own file—in the quiet and safe environment of Father Doheny's chambers. He could help her piece it all together. Then she'd take her new identity and move on, leaving everything behind. That was what she'd told herself over and over all day—that was—until he kissed her.

In those few moments she remembered their night together. The way he made her feel. How he and he alone was the first man who ever made her think she could ever live a normal life—a happily ever after.

Jane shook it all off and reminded herself of the photos of him in the NSA file. Chumming up to Three, tagged as a known conspirator. The thought of him aiding the man she hated the most, the man who'd made her life a living hell, who'd been behind the deaths of Havis and her friend Jen—*this* was the man he'd associated himself with? The man he was aiding and abetting? No. Not on Jane's watch. She needed to do what she did best—turn her feelings off. Clearly there was a reason Crow had sent her the kill assignment. Now, she needed to do her job.

Jane watched the front doors of the massive white building with the Corinthian columns. It was like a scene from a Hollywood movie—that is, if the movie was set in Rome. She thought it ostentatious and bold of the company to look so *rich* knowing it was charging the U.S. government over twelve million dollars apiece for each drone it sold. Granted they got the job done, but now that she'd seen the American-made product in the hands and the garage of Six in Queens, N.Y., and Matt in photos yucking it up with Three,

Jane wondered where else Maxtronix drones had found a home.

The main entrance swung open and Matt Matthews walked onto the front steps of the building. Stopping in the darkness, he surveyed the parking lot, looking her way. Jane ducked behind a massive oak tree—one of many on the grounds. There was no way he could see her. It was too dark and she was stealthy. She watched him take a deep cleansing breath of the fresh night air, turn around and key-card his way back into the building.

Shaking her head, Jane stood upright behind the tree where she'd been crouching. "What the hell?" She'd wait longer. It wouldn't be the first time she'd sat outside all night waiting to kill a man.

Turning her back slightly, she sat on the Max HQ grounds and leaned her head against the massive tree. The turf felt like a golf course beneath her fingertips and the entire lawn smelled of sweet Bermuda. The scent of freshly cut grass wafted on the breeze, but the entire campus reeked of money. When Jane first met Matt, he was old money doing his best to act like he wasn't. It was a trait Jane didn't have a hard time recognizing in him or others. When you grew up with nothing, it was easy to peg who was raised with money and who wasn't. Those who had it acted one of two ways. They either had a silver spoon so far up their ass you could see their elitist attitude from forty paces, or they looked a like a homeless person but still possessed impeccable manners. On the flip side, there were the people who grew up with nothing, then earned their wealth. They appreciated everything they owned and were easy to spot. They took care of their prized possessions. Their cars, their boats, even their clothes—all of the *things* they never had growing up were front and center and were showpieces. People with old money wrecked their cars and didn't give a shit. Material things didn't matter, because there would always be more. New money folks worried it could all go away—they still remembered what it was like to be hungry. And then there were those with no money—ever. Most of the time they were normal, hard-working folks who couldn't catch a break or seem to get ahead. But every now and then there would be the ones who'd work the system. Those who'd take on foster kids like

Jane. Not to care for a kid in need, but for the paycheck. Jane knew there were good parents in the foster care system—she'd just never been lucky enough to cross their path.

Jane had paid her dues and now her millions were sitting in a bank in Switzerland. She'd earned every penny. What she would do with the money, she had no idea. Money held no real value for her. She'd learned to live without it and off the grid for so long, she had no concept of what joy or pleasure the money might afford her.

She ticked through these thoughts aimlessly and watched the front door, waiting for Matt to re-emerge into the dark, night sky.

"What are you doing out here?"

Jane got to her feet in an instant, the syringes of midazolam and succinylcholine shoved deep into the back pockets of her jeans. Jane said nothing.

"Did you hear me?" Matt asked again, his eyes sparkling in the light cast from the illuminated columns on the front of the building.

"Where did you come from?"

Matt cocked his head. "These trees have

eyes." Matt pointed up but didn't take his gaze from Jane. "I've been watching you from inside, wondering if you were going to come to the front door and knock. Say, *hey Matt. It's me. How are you? Sorry I skipped out on you in Atlanta. Sorry I walked away again today after Collie's funeral.*"

Jane put her hands behind her back, reaching for the syringes.

"Keep your hands were I can see them," Matt said. "Call me crazy, but I've seen what you can do to a man, to *more* than one man for that matter, and after today when someone whispered into my ear *she's coming to kill you*, I've been a little on edge."

Jane showed her hands to Matt. "What?" The question uncontrollably slipped out of her mouth.

"Oh yeah," Matt continued as he moved in closer. "*She's coming to kill you and I can't help you again*, were his exact words."

Jane blanched. Who would warn him? Who would know?

"Tell me who you are—who you *really* are—and why you're out here waiting for me. Are you here to kill me?" Matt asked the question calmly, but it was clear from the look on his face he was rattled.

"Who are *you*, Matt Matthews?" Jane asked. "You told me you were a reporter. I think we both know that's not true."

"I think we're both guilty of telling some untruths, don't you? How about this, you show me yours and I'll show you mine."

Jane said nothing. A hundred scenarios ran through her head. She could take him at any moment. What was holding her back?

"Tell me who you really are, Matt. Are you aiding and abetting the Islamic State?"

Matt shook his head. "No. Are you?"

Jane bristled. "No."

"So we're even. Neither of us is the bad guy."

Jane stared deep into Matt's eyes. Who *was* the man standing in front of her? She knew evil like it was her best friend and Matt Matthews *wasn't* evil—not at all. He'd never given off that sense of all-encompassing selfishness that was evil's closest companion. Or was their night in bed clouding her assessment of him? Her fantasies of him? Her memories of his naked body lying on top of hers? Was this impairing her usual straightforward judgement? Whatever it was, Jane wasn't thinking clearly. She couldn't complete a kill with a muddled head. Not here. Not tonight.

"Please," Matt said, stepping closer to her. "Just tell me who you are."

Jane didn't shy away from him. She needed to bring him in. She needed to make him more vulnerable. She licked her mouth with nervous energy, then bit down on the thickness of her red, bottom lip. She watched him visibly sigh and the corner of his mouth turn up—almost twitch in anticipation.

"I like the blonde hair, by the way."

Jane forced a smile.

Matt moved in closer. Jane allowed it.

"Just talk to me. *Please.* I don't know who you are and frankly, I don't care. To me, you're the woman who saved my life and ... rocked my world. I've thought of nothing but you since that night." Matt inched closer, his eyes seemed desperate with want and a need for acceptance. "I saw you in New York. You ran from me in the subway. Why? I even saw you with that guy—the redheaded musclebound meathead. It killed me to watch you kiss him. It *killed* me," he said, looking up to the sky, his jealousy so obviously spilling out. "If you ever looked at me once with what I *know* is in your heart, I would—"

"What?" Jane asked.

"I'd be your slave. I'd follow you anywhere just to be with you."

Matt gripped Jane's elbows, her hands now hanging by her sides. She stared at his steely eyes and mussed and curly hair. Nothing in her years of training prepared her for this. Her order, for the first time in her career, was in direct conflict with her gut—or maybe it was her heart. This was the man she was supposed to kill?

"Talk to me," he said. "Say something. *Anything.*"

"Are you working with Siad al Daleel ul Khyayraat or any other member of the Islamic State?"

Matt shook his head, then leaned it into Jane's forehead. "No. You have to believe me. I can't tell you how or why, but I'm a patriot. I swear to you, for better or worse, my allegiance lies with the United States of America."

Without another word, Matt Matthews took Jane's face in his hands and kissed her.

Not wasting precious time, he parted her lips with his tongue and swept her mouth. Jane lost focus—momentarily. She wrapped her arms around his neck and pulled him near, kissing him deeply. Matt let out a small moan as Jane led them both down and to the soft grass. Lying on top of him, Jane reached into her right back pocket, freeing the syringe of the sedative.

He unzipped her jacket, running his warm hand between her breasts before lifting the white tank top up and over her bra. Rolling them both over, Matt lay on top of her, kissing his way down her tight and muscular stomach. Jane tugged at his rumpled shirt with one hand, pulling it still buttoned over his head and tossing it to the side.

Jane ran her hand down Matt's tan chest as he stared into her eyes. She blinked slowly through a hooded gaze, watching him drink her in. "God, you're beautiful," he said. "Do you have any idea how many times I dreamt of you and me together again? The night you left, I had this amazing dream we were on the beach," he said, leaning down to kiss her neck. "Pink sands. Bermuda. We were sunburnt and in love."

Jane's breath hitched and Matt took it as his cue to kiss her again. He did.

Jane fidgeted with the button on his khaki pants. He fully complied, helping her unzip the pants himself. Already hard, he pressed against her still clothed body and kissed her deeply, passionately.

Jane gripped the syringe, her thumb flat against the plunger. Into the grass, she expelled most of the midazolam. Matt pulled away from her and gazed into her eyes. "Let's get out of here. I want you, but I don't want to do this on the lawn."

"Do what?"

Matt pushed the uneven blonde locks from Jane's face. "Look, I don't know why I'm saying this." He looked away for a split second then back to her. "Actually, I *do* know. It's when your life falls apart that you have clarity, and I'm seeing things so much clearer—more clear than ever before. I'm completely uncertain about nearly every aspect of my life right now—every part of it except one. *You.*"

Matt took a beat—a breath as if he was ramping up to something.

"I'm falling in love with you. There. I said

it. My life is *shit*—complete shit and I have no idea what will happen in the future but I know one thing—I want you in it. I know that's not romantic and as I say it out loud I'm sure it doesn't sound even remotely appealing. I mean, why would anyone want to join this circus? And that's exactly what I'm asking you to do. But I can see so clearly and I know it as plain as the nose on my face. I—want—you. I want to take care of you, love you, take you to the best places on earth, have a life with you, grow old and grey with you. And that all starts now. C'mon," he said, leaning in for one final kiss. "Let's go."

Jane had listened without interrupting. His sincere and honest confession had left her breathless. Still, she took the opportunity, knowing it would be her last. With his face against hers, she squeezed her eyes shut and plunged the needle into his neck, giving him just enough sedative to knock him out cold.

Rearing back at the sting of the needle, shock filled his eyes before they rolled back in his head. Matt collapsed on top of her. Jane let out a heartbroken sigh.

DAY TWO | 2310 HOURS

JANE ROARED DOWN the highway on the Harley through Arlington toward Eve's Court in Columbia Heights. She was sexually frustrated, amped up and ready to either fuck or kill someone—and not necessarily in that order.

After drugging Matt, she'd redressed him, then propped him against the tree. It would be another two or three hours before he would be conscious again, unless someone found him. She knew he would wake up mad—but mad was better than dead, which was her original plan. Jane had never aborted a kill—*never.* She'd also never slept with one of her assignments. She'd now passed on two golden opportunities to complete her mission.

I'm falling in love with you.

Jane couldn't get the words out of her head as the night air hung low and a fog began to roll in from across the Potomac. If Jane couldn't kill Matt, she knew who she *could* eliminate. *Four.* He wasn't her assignment, but she was taking him out all the same. This was her last rodeo. It was time. She would take her file—her lost life and *get lost*. Start over. Find herself somehow in the past and start anew.

As she rumbled through the night air on the Harley, Matt's *other* words haunted her. It wasn't that he'd been told *she's been sent to kill you*, but he'd been specifically told, *I can't help you again.* The words rang true to Jane. She'd been told the same thing. Those *exact* words. Someone *would* be coming for her. She knew it.

She pulled onto Fourteenth Street and stared up at the second floor apartment that belonged to Four. It was dark and Jane hoped it meant he wasn't home. She'd set up an ambush, kill him when he arrived, and leave.

Looking at the time, Jane realized how late it had become. Just past eleven, it would be hard to find someone coming into the building. She could pick the lock on Four's apartment door, but she couldn't get past the security key card entry so easily. She'd need to walk in with a tenant. That meant more waiting outside and the temperature had started to drop. All Jane had to keep her warm was her hoodie and the thought of Matt feeling her up in the bushes.

A slow fifteen minutes passed and Jane was beginning to think her plan to burn off her frustration wasn't going to work out. But then it happened. A rusted out Toyota pulled up in front of the building. Burning oil, it sputtered to a halt. Out jumped a delivery boy with what looked to be Chinese food. Jane casually took to the sidewalk, hanging back far enough for him to hit the call button and speak to whomever wanted eggdrop soup at eleven-thirty at night.

When he was buzzed in, Jane whisked past him with a quick *thanks* and took to the stairs, climbing them two by two to the second floor.

Four's apartment was at the end of the U-shaped building. Jane looked up and down the hall before pulling her tools—a rake and a hook—from the side pocket of her backpack. It only took five seconds and she was in, the lock snapping open with a crack.

Letting herself in, Jane shut the door without a sound and searched the apartment. Four wasn't home. Truth be told, she was a little disappointed. She could've shot him up in bed and the old boy would've never woken up again. Now, she'd be forced to wait on him.

In the meantime, Jane took the opportunity to look around. Turning on the Maglite she kept in her backpack, she walked to the kitchenette in the small dining area. Covered with papers, she knew the drill. These guys were notorious for leaving their stuff lying about. They were sloppy—arrogant—untouchable. At least they thought so until the very end when Jane was staring them in the face.

The notes were in Arabic but understandable. It was a map of the Capitol building—the Hall of Representatives, the Senate Chamber, the Rotunda, Old Hall of Representatives and the Supreme Court. The drawings were old. In fact, they almost looked original to the building. Jane shook her head. "This can't be good," she whispered.

Under the blueprints were requisition orders for uniforms. Uniforms for United States Capitol Police, security guards and custodians. This was well-thought out. It wasn't three guys in matching down coats with dirty bombs in the subway. This was a coordinated attack with several *inside* players. And they were hitting where they thought it would disrupt the American way of life—our government.

Jane searched through the material, memorizing as many names and places as she could get through. *His* name was on each and every document and her blood boiled each time she had to see it. *Three.*

So embroiled in the intel she'd uncovered, Jane didn't hear the men speaking in the hallway. She was even more surprised when the lights came on in the apartment.

Turning, she faced Four head on. Two paces behind him walked Three.

"What are you doing in here?" Four shouted, waving his arms about frantically. "*What are you doing in here?*"

Three said nothing, but met her eye to eye once again. The man's gaze caught her off guard and he stared her down as if he knew her beyond their meeting in Atlanta.

Jane turned on a dime, throwing open the sliding glass door to the balcony. With a running start, she jumped the two stories to the grassy lawn below, rolling out of the fall before coming to her feet and taking off at dead run and into the cover of the bushes. She was out of sight and catching her breath when she saw Three calmly walk onto the balcony—the sheer curtains blowing in the cool night air. He took a deep breath in through his nose, flaring his nostrils. Faintly in the darkness, Jane heard him say it. "We will meet again."

DAY THREE | ZERO DARK THIRTY

J ANE'S HEART RACED and her ankle ached as she kick-started the Harley and sped down Fourteenth Street to the Jambo. She needed to stash the bike, take a breath and eat some food. She was shaken, tired, out of sorts. It wasn't like her to be so *off.* Jane knew for the first time in her career with Coywolf or anywhere else—she was slipping. She wasn't the machine she needed to be, but something else. Something or someone with feelings and emotions that kept bubbling to the surface. Emotions that kept her from being the instrument of execution she was known to be. Jane didn't like it. She'd learned long ago to tamp that shit down. Father Doheny always said she packed away her feelings in boxes high on a shelf in an imaginary closet. She only got them down when she wanted. Even though she'd never allowed anyone into *the closet*, it somehow felt like people were getting into her *boxes*—opening them. Or maybe, she'd somehow left her closet door open.

Relieved to have the Jambo in her sights, she parked the Harley in the back of the small hotel and hurried to the front of the building. Still high on adrenaline from her encounter with Three and Four, Jane fumbled with her backpack as she dug to the bottom for the two keys Claire had given her. Her hands shook and she stopped to clench her fists and calm herself.

He was on her before she knew what happened, her hands cuffed behind her back and her backpack and keys at her feet before she could react. "What the fuck?" Jane winced in pain as her shoulder wrenched out of place.

"Stay calm. I only want to talk to you. Now, how do we get inside this little hotel? Is there a key in your backpack?"

He turned her body, not letting go of the handcuffs for even a moment. Jane stared into the blue eyes of Kelly Casey and shook her head in disgust. Rage filled her body from the tips of her toes to the top of her head. Her first instinct was to head butt him. She refrained, saving her wrath for later when she could unleash it properly. Instead, Jane said nothing, her backpack now at her feet, the keys thankfully spilled onto the wooden porch. She took a breath, kicked the keys toward him and formulated a plan.

"Are these the keys?" Kelly asked.

Jane rolled her eyes in disgust and nodded.

He picked them up along with her backpack and slipped the key into the lock, opening the door. Taking Jane by the arm, he escorted her through the front door, shutting it behind them. "Where are we going?" he asked in a whisper.

Jane looked at the staircase with only her eyes. Kelly slung the backpack over his shoulder and proceeded to guide her up the stairs. "No funny business, okay? Take me to your room. I'll get you out of the cuffs. We need to talk."

Jane walked without resisting, stopping in front of her door. Still, she remained silent. Kelly took the second key on the keyring and opened the door to Jane's room. Flipping the switch on the wall, the room illuminated via the antique lamp by the bed. A warm, yellow glow enveloped them.

"This is nice," Kelly remarked. "Quaint."

Closing the door, he sat Jane on the bed and went back to lock the door, sliding the chain lock into place. Facing Jane, he put on what Jane called the pleasant and reassuring cop face—a fake smile. "I only want to talk to you—I *need* to talk to you. And you have to listen to me. The only way I knew to accomplish that was to get you up here alone. If I'd confronted you *outside*, you would've run away or," he hesitated as he looked at her. "God only knows what else. Now," he said exhaling. "You stole my keys, broke into my apartment and unlocked my safe." Kelly crossed his arms across his chest. The tattoo of Saint Michael the Archangel crept out from under the dark blue T-shirt he wore—the sleeves tight around his solid biceps. "We *really* need to talk," he added for emphasis.

Jane stared at him, blinking. She said nothing.

"I'm going to take off the cuffs, and then we're going to have a chat like civilized human beings. There's some important stuff we need to go over. About—you and about me."

Jane stared at him, not making a move.

"Look, I need you to say something—acknowledge me in some way because I know your name's not Alice Hart."

Blood rushed to Jane's cheeks. It was obvious Kelly saw the emotion painted on her face. He made his move to unlock the cuffs.

Jane, still jacked from her near-sex/death encounter with Matt, coupled with getting nailed by Three *and* Four before escaping out a second floor balcony, had more adrenaline pumping through her veins than Kelly Casey could have ever anticipated. With one hand out of the cuffs, Jane junk-punched Kelly in the balls with a left uppercut, taking him to his knees before promptly snapping the empty cuff around his wrist. Then, taking the key from his shaking hand, she released herself and cuffed Kelly to the sturdy oak bedframe.

When she was done, she stood back and surveyed her handiwork like she'd just roped a calf in record time at a rodeo. Kelly lay on the side of the bed, grabbing his crotch with his one free hand and moaning in pain.

"C'mon," Jane whined. "I didn't hit you *that* hard."

"*Fuuuuuuck.*"

Jane looked at him for only a moment, pursed her lips then picked up a chair from across the room and brought it to sit beside the bed. Turning it around, she straddled it, crossing her arms over the top to stare at Kelly Casey.

When he finally stopped moaning and wiped his watering eyes, Kelly sat up and made a strange, twisted face. "I'm gonna vomit."

Jane blanched. "Not on my bed you're not."

"I'm serious," he mumbled.

"*Really?*" Jane kicked her leg over the chair and hustled to the bathroom for the plastic wastebasket. She got it to Kelly not a moment too soon. He puked as soon as she handed it to him, his shoulders heaving with each horrid retch of his body—his huge arm cradling the round trash can like a lover.

She sat back down in the chair, turning her head to stay downwind. Jane could slit a man's throat and watch him bleed out, shoot a man between the eyes and witness his brain matter hit the wall behind him—hell, she could even blow a man apart with a grenade, but seeing a man throw up turned her stomach. "Ew," she groused. "Are you finished?"

Kelly nodded, wiping his mouth with the back of his hand. Jane took the trash can and flushed its contents down the toilet, gagging the entire time. She returned with a wet washcloth and handed it to Kelly. Then, searching through her backpack, she found her hand sanitizer. Globbing it into her palm, she wrung her hands over and over then took her place on the chair once again.

"You wanna tell me who you are?" Kelly asked, wiping his face and mouth with the damp cloth.

Jane gave him a crooked smile and shook her head. "You first, Captain Puke Pants. How do you know *anything* about me?"

"I know a *lot* about you. *Jane. Jane Doe.*"

The smug expression fell from Jane's face and she rose from the chair and turned her back on Kelly, facing the door.

"You can run away if you want," he said. "But it won't change who you are. It won't change who I am, or the fact my father saved your life the night you were born. Did you know you spent your first night out of the hospital in *my* house—*my* crib? That's right. You spent your first night in the real world with *me*, Jane. That's gotta count for something."

A wave of panic-filled emotion overcame her. Jane felt as if she was hovering above, watching herself receive the news from Kelly. Her eyes welled with feelings she didn't understand—emotions she didn't know how to navigate. It was a mental state she was ill-equipped to manage. A single tear fell from her eye, landing on the old hardwood floor in a splash. Her body shook, the rush too much for her to handle. The ringing in her ears was deafening, and although she knew Kelly was saying something, she had no idea what it was. It all sounded muted, booming from deep inside a well.

Please, take the cuffs off so I can help you. So I can explain what I know. You deserve that. His words echoed in a distant place and her feet seemed cemented to the floor—her legs too heavy to move.

"Jane? Can you hear me? Jesus, I think you're going into shock and I'm cuffed to this goddamned bed."

Kelly struggled against the headboard. His tight muscles strained against the tenacity of the oak. Finally, the glue holding the spindle to the main headboard gave way under his power and at once the handcuff came free. Pulling the splintered wood from the silver cuff, he rushed to Jane's side, holding her from behind.

"Talk to me, Jane."

She turned to look at him. Pale, her eyes rolled back in her head. Collapsing in Kelly's arms, he carried her to the bed. Laying her down, he propped up her legs and feet and covered her with the heavy quilt. "Jane, I need you to talk to me. I *know* you don't want me to call EMS so I need you to stay with me. Listen to me. You have to pull it together. Pull your *shit* together Jane." Kelly lifted her head and stared into her lifeless face. *"Damn it Jane!"*

Batting her lashes, Jane looked into Kelly's eyes and scowled.

"There she is," he said, his signature toothy grin spreading from ear to ear. "I thought I'd lost you for a second.

Jane tried to sit up. The room began to spin. Coming to her feet, she stumbled to the bathroom, running into the doorframe and falling to her knees in front of the toilet. Retching, she threw up until there was nothing left inside her body, then began to dry-heave.

Kelly stood over her, holding back her hair. When she was finished, Jane sat back on her butt and placed her head in her hands.

"*Really?*" Kelly joked, handing her a clean washcloth.

She gazed up at him with only her eyes. Jane said nothing.

Kelly slid down onto the bathroom floor next to her. The cold white tiles were missing in places and the old claw foot tub needed to be re-glazed—small things no one would notice unless they were up close and personal. Jane and Kelly were. It was a starting place for both of them.

"Are you okay?" Kelly asked, placing his hand on her knee.

Jane stared at him and blinked hard. She swallowed the emotion that kept gurgling up in her throat. There was nothing left in her stomach. She blinked back the tears welling in her eyes.

"Look, I know this is a lot. But I want to

help. I've waited my whole life to—"

Kelly brushed his fingers down her jean covered shin, bringing them back up to rest on her knee. "To find you. My dad…my dad spent his entire career looking for you, Jane. And now."

Jane stood abruptly and walked out of the bathroom, leaving Kelly and his sentimental walk down memory lane alone on the cold tile floor.

Digging through her backpack, Jane pulled out a toothbrush and toothpaste and came back to the bathroom, turning on the water. Without giving Kelly a second glance, she began to brush.

Kelly came to his feet. Standing behind her, he watched her reflection in the mirror. Jane kept her eyes down, completely engaged in the brushing of her teeth. "I know why you chase him. I do," Kelly said.

Jane spit, rinsed and shook the excess water from the toothbrush. She wiped her mouth and exited the bathroom, leaving Kelly alone again.

"Will you listen to me?" he asked, following her.

Jane shoved the toothbrush and toothpaste

back into her bag—the bag that contained everything she owned. She stared down at it. She'd spent her entire life living out of *a bag*. Whether it was a plastic garbage bag she'd lug from place to place as a foster kid or a ruck sack as a Marine, she was once again living out of just the backpack—running from place to place. Now it was all falling apart in grand fashion.

Jane pulled the police file from the backpack and turned to face Kelly, holding it in her hands like she'd placed it on a silver platter.

Kelly glanced down at it and then back to her. "You stole that from me. Do you know what it's like to have your keys stolen from your car in front of your entire unit? It's embarrassing as hell."

Jane spoke for the first time. "I'm sorry."

Kelly nodded and shifted his weight nervously before crossing his arms against his tight chest. "Apology accepted."

Jane stared at the file folder. "I thought when I took it that night that I would open it right away. I thought I'd go through it with a fine-toothed comb—read every last note. I always told myself if I ever had the chance to know what happened, where I came from and how I ended up the way I did, I would—" Jane stopped cold.

"You'd what?"

She shook her head. "I don't know."

Kelly took a deep breath. "Look, I *know* why you're chasing him. I know why you track him. My question is, did you kill Al-Sistani to get to him?"

Jane pulled her attention from the closed police file back to Kelly. "What are you talking about?"

Kelly walked to her, took the file from her hands and sat down on the bed, carefully cradling his balls and wincing. Jane followed. "At first I thought you were working with the Islamic State. I never bought the whole *I'm a writer* story," Kelly began.

Jane let out a small, unconvincing laugh. "Why?"

"Because I'm a cop and I'm paid *not* to take people at face value."

Jane rolled her eyes at him.

"I came to see you and you had bruised knuckles. I had two known members of the militant Islamic State on their way to the hospital and a group of women who've been held hostage for thirty days singing the praises of *Malaekah*—the angel who rescued them. Not to mention an old man at the church you drugged and then—"

"Then what, Kelly?" Jane calmly asked.

"You fucking slayed Al-Sistani. With a damn helicopter. Why? To make it look like an accident?"

"Kelly—"

"Look, I'm not mad. There was some bad shit about to go down with those boys. You did us all a favor."

Jane looked away, one corner of her mouth turned up.

"I guess you knew that too, huh?"

Jane looked back to him but said nothing.

"Anyway," Kelly continued. "You broke into my apartment."

Jane raised one eyebrow. "I used your keys."

"You *stole* from me."

"What was *mine* in the first place."

They stared at the police file that lay between them on the bed as they sat on either side. "It was my *father's*, but now that you have what you want, I feel like I can put some of the pieces of your story together. Like I said, now I *know* why you track him."

"*What* in the hell are you *talking* about?" Jane asked.

"You *really* haven't looked inside this?"

Jane shook her head.

"*Jane*," Kelly sighed, ripping off the rubber band that held the worn file together. Jane watched as Kelly shuffled through stacks and stacks of handwritten notes and reports. She saw an autopsy report, a copy of her birth certificate—one that wasn't like her own—there were timetables, maps, photographs of crime scenes—even one of the dumpster where she was found. Jane placed her hand on top of Kelly's and stopped him when he came to a five by seven black and white photo. Long dark hair and light eyes, Jane lifted the photograph to the light for a better look. Kelly paused his frantic search and watched Jane as she gazed upon the image of the beautiful twenty-something woman.

Kelly swallowed hard. "That's—"

"I know who she is," Jane whispered staring at the nose and high cheek bones that resembled her own. "She's my mother."

Kelly looked back to the pile on the bed. His shoulders dropped. Everything lying in front of them wasn't merely the paper trail from a case. It might've looked like photos, scraps and Post-it notes, but to Jane, it was her entire life. "Her name was, Dessa," Kelly said. "Dessa Ellison."

Jane held onto the photograph as Kelly continued his search. "Dessa Ellison." Jane breathed her name into the universe as if she'd never existed before that very moment.

"Here," he said, pulling a piece of yellow legal paper from the pile. It was a handwritten note dated April 5, 1988. At the top it read *Possible Suspects*. There had been a list of five. Three were marked through with a black pen. Two remained. One was circled with a star next to it.

"*Jane*," Kelly said, trying to get her attention. "This is what I'm talking about."

Jane pulled her eyes away from the photo of her mother to look at the paper.

"My dad went through every possible suspect for your mother's killer."

"He *knew* who the killer was?"

Kelly leaned into Jane, touching her on the shoulder. "You seriously haven't looked at *any* of this?"

Jane swallowed hard, the bile in her stomach rising to meet her throat once more. She spoke, barely getting the word out. "No."

Kelly let out a nervous sigh. "I thought you were tracking him because of this."

"Stop talking in circles, Kelly, and tell me what in the hell you're trying to say."

"*This.*" Kelly said, slamming the paper down in front of Jane, pointing to the name circled and starred. "Dad's number one suspect. Dale Khyayraat. A.K.A. Siad al Daleel ul Khyayraat."

Jane gasped. The world inside the tiny hotel room collapsed around her.

DAY THREE | 0315 HOURS

MATT AWOKE, HIS mouth dry and hanging open, fully clothed but disheveled. Wiping the drool from his chapped lips, he did his best to stand. Still unsure of where he was or what was happening, he looked at his watch. It was three fifteen in the morning. He picked a leaf from his hair and leaned against the nearby oak tree, piecing together what he *could* remember of the last few hours.

His wallet, keys and phone were all in his pockets. He remembered working with Peter in the lab. He remembered seeing the micro-drones. Matt rubbed his head, shaking the cobwebs from his mind. He stared at the full moon and spied one of the hidden cameras and recalled how he came to be on the front property.

"What the hell did she give me?" Matt

asked aloud, now rubbing his neck and the injection site. Still groggy, he wandered out of the darkened and wooded area and into the Maxtronix parking lot. Pausing at the door of his car, he stopped to think of the words whispered to him in the cemetery. *She's been sent to kill you. Leave town. Get out now. I can't help you again.*

She'd been waiting in the woods to end his life. Matt unlocked his car and slid into the driver's seat. Flipping the visor down, the light illuminated and he got a good look at the injection mark on his neck. If she'd wanted to kill him, she certainly could have. She didn't.

Matt started the car and put it in reverse to leave. He'd already decided he was checking into a hotel. There was no way in hell he was going back to his father's place. Pulling up to security, he was met by an armed guard. "Working late tonight, Mr. Matthews?"

Matt caught a glimpse of himself in the side mirror. He looked like forty miles of bad road. He wasn't fooling anyone into thinking he'd been working. He looked like he'd been sleeping on the side lawn—which was exactly what he'd been doing. "It was a long day."

"Yes sir. I liked General Collins very much sir. You have my deepest condolences."

The gate opened and Matt nodded. "Thank you."

As he pulled out onto the highway in his aging BMW, the front pocket of his wrinkled khaki's silently buzzed. Matt had no idea who would be calling him in the middle of the night but his first thought was *her*.

He dug the phone from his pocket, stretching his leg into the floorboard and taking his foot off the gas for a moment. It was an unknown caller. "Matthews."

A series of clicks followed and a knot formed in the pit of Matt's stomach. It was an all too familiar sound—one he'd heard many times. Still, he waited.

"Matt Matthews?"

Matt hesitated a moment before identifying himself. "Yes."

A long pause took over the airwaves. So long that Matt found himself confirming the call was still connected. "Hello?"

"Proceed to the Hay-Adams Hotel. Eight hundred, Sixteenth Street. Tomorrow. Oh-eight-hundred-hours. Ask for John Smith at the front desk. Wait in your room for further instructions."

With a *click*, the line went dead.

Matt tossed his phone into the passenger's seat. He'd called in days ago and asked to come out and had been told to stand down. To wait. They'd be in touch with further instructions. Now he had them.

Matt sped through the night toward downtown D.C. If he was expected to be at the Hay-Adams in five hours, he was staying there tonight. He'd check in on his own and go to the front desk in the morning.

His suitcase was in the backseat but it didn't contain much. Matt had already exhausted the clothes he'd packed. He'd learned to travel light, which in turn meant he was a man of very few possessions. He did however, still have the suit he'd worn to Collie's funeral. With a new shirt from the gift shop in the Hay-Adams lobby, he'd be presentable enough for his debriefing.

He had a few things to get off his mind and a few questions he'd like to ask—like since when did number Three on *The List* become a protected informant?

DAY THREE | 0600 HOURS

JANE OPENED HER eyes. Her head was deeply nestled into the pillows of the bed and she was securely under the covers. Feeling up and down her body, she knew she was wearing only her tank top and panties. Snapping her head from side to side, she quickly checked to see if she was in the bed alone. Across the room, sitting at the desk was, Kelly Casey—shirtless, his jeans unbuttoned at the top—he was awake and sifting through stacks of paper. With each movement of his arms, Jane could see his sinewy back shift, his muscles flexing and relaxing over and over. The tattoo of Saint Michael seemed to glow off his arm and tight body in the morning light.

Jane sat up, rubbing the sleep from her eyes. "What the hell?"

Kelly turned, the chair letting out a moan

under his weight. Standing, he hitched up the sagging jeans that showed off the muscular V of his waistline. Taking the t-shirt from the back of the chair, he slipped it over his head, digging his way through the armholes as he walked toward her. "How are you feeling?" he asked, sitting on the bed next to her.

"What happened?"

"Well," Kelly said with an edge of sarcasm to his voice. "When was the last time you ate something?"

Jane closed one eye and twisted her face. "Honestly? I don't remember. I take so little interest in my daily life that I hardly think to eat and drink."

"I believe we may have found your problem, Miss Doe. You're suffering from a case of extremely low blood sugar, coupled with acute stress."

Jane didn't look at him, although she could feel his eyes all over her. "You wanna tell me how I got out of my clothes?"

Kelly shrugged. "I only wanted you to be as comfortable as possible."

"So you took my clothes off?" she asked, finally catching his gaze squarely.

Kelly smiled, unable to hide his toothy grin. "Let's face it. It's not like I haven't taken your clothes off before. Although I must say, the first time was a hell of a lot more fun."

"Why? Because I was conscious?"

Kelly put his arm around her naked shoulder and pulled her into his strong and capable body, then placed a sweet kiss on the top of her head. He wasn't the same man who'd cuffed her just hours earlier. "No. Because you were taking mine off too."

"Ugh." Jane cried out and slid her bottom off the bed, walking toward the bathroom. "I need a shower."

"You need food."

She turned and faced him. "I *need* to brush my teeth and then I need to go over every last bit of paper in my police file."

"It's *my* police file."

Jane stood in the doorway of the bathroom in only her white tank top and panties. Her small frame was thin, but deceiving. Even at her tiniest, she still managed to subdue all six foot two, two hundred-plus pounds of Kelly the night before, handcuffing him to the headboard—and not in a good way. She gave him one last glare before slamming the door.

"And I *used* your toothbrush!" Kelly shouted.

———————

SITTING AT THE diner across the street from the Jambo, Kelly and Jane took turns passing the folder back and forth.

"Siad was a student at Pitt from 1984 to 1988. His parents were wealthy and wanted their boy to have an American education," Kelly said. "My father thought he and Dessa knew each other from school."

"My mom went to Pitt."

Kelly nodded.

"When he interviewed her friends—" Jane began.

"It's all in here, they didn't even know she was pregnant. But they *did* say she knew him. They had a of couple classes together."

"She knew him," Jane repeated in a breathless tone.

"She'd been to a study group the night prior to the murder—a study group *he* was a part of. They didn't leave together, but apparently they weren't getting along too well."

"Why?" Jane asked.

"An eyewitness saw them arguing, but you won't find the testimony in the file. When push came to shove, the guy recanted his story."

"Let me guess," Jane said, already knowing the answer to her question.

Kelly rubbed his fingers to his thumb. "Money talks and bullshit walks."

"Any DNA evidence?"

"There *was*. It was destroyed. Like I said, once Dad started digging in too deep, stuff went missing, like where *you* were in the foster care system. He swore they lost you on purpose."

Jane's eyes widened in agreement. "I was lost all right. Lost somewhere between one shitty foster home and another."

"You seemed to have come out with some skills," Kelly said, raising a suspicious eyebrow.

"What do you mean?"

"Do you know how I found you in D.C.?"

Jane shook her head.

"I knew you'd be tracking Siad. I called a friend in the Secret Service and she pulled some strings and gave me his last known whereabouts. I went there, and lo and behold, who did I see? *You*, jumping from a second floor apartment building, hopping on a Harley I'd stake my life is hotter than a hooker's panties on a Saturday night, and taking off through the streets of Columbia Heights like your ass was on fire."

Jane shrugged and took a swig of the Pedia-lyte Kelly had stopped to buy her at the corner drugstore, then nonchalantly looked over her shoulder as if she was impatient for her breakfast. She wasn't.

"You wanna tell me about it?"

Jane said nothing.

The waitress showed up with a pencil behind her ear and their breakfast order in her hands. "Who ordered the Big Country, eggs over medium with wheat toast and bacon?"

Kelly pointed to Jane and she placed the other plate in front of him. "Eat, Jane. You can't run on empty anymore. Not if we're going to get him."

Jane looked to her eggs and then immediately into Kelly's eyes with a suspicious smile. "What do you mean *we*?"

"I've kept this file all these years, finally

found you and he's *this* close? I want him, Jane. I want him and I want him prosecuted."

Jane scoffed and began peppering her eggs. She took one bite and then buttered her toast. "I got this, *Sergeant Casey*. Okay?"

"Don't patronize me, Jane. Look, I know you're probably not going to give up whatever it is you do," he said, wiggling his fingers in mocking quotations. "But you know what *I* do? I find and prosecute terrorists. And that's what he is. A terrorist." Kelly washed his first bite of breakfast down with a gulp of coffee.

Jane opened the file folder and stared into the eyes of her beautiful mother. She wondered what her life would've been like if her mother had lived—if she hadn't been tossed from foster home to foster home—treated like a dog. "You know," Jane began, easily disconnecting from thoughts of her childhood as she always had. "It's funny you should say that."

"Say what?"

"That second floor apartment I jumped from last night? Inside it were plans. Architectural plans of the Capitol Building—in particular the Hall of Representatives, the Senate Chamber, the Rotunda and the Supreme

Court. Not to mention requisition orders for uniforms. Everything from Capitol Police to janitorial service. Something big is going down, so I think it's ironic you find and prosecute terrorists for a living."

"What are you talking about? Who knows about this?" he asked, now sitting on the edge of his seat.

Jane gritted her teeth and ignored his question. "I think it's ironic you find and prosecute terrorists for a living because I find and *kill* them for a living. And that's exactly what I'm going to do to him." Jane leaned into the table and lowered her voice. "I'm going to kill Siad al Daleel ul Khyayraat—The Instructor—Number Three on *The List* if it's the last thing I ever do on this earth."

Kelly paused and without reaction or expression, he replied. "Okay. I'm in."

DAY THREE | 0650 HOURS

MATT STEPPED OUT of the hotel shower and onto the cold marble floor. He estimated he'd actually slept two of the three hours he'd tossed and turned in the king-sized bed with the beautiful view of the White House—mostly because whatever *she'd* shot him up with was still running its course through his system.

Sliding his palm across the foggy mirror, Matt leaned into his reflection for a closer look. His face, once tan, was now faded—a distant memory of his past life. The dark circles under his eyes told the story of his *new* life—one of stress and grief. He wrapped a towel around his waist, the water still dripping from his body, and ran his hands through his hair, combing it back as best he could. It would be the extent of his personal grooming for the day. Lifting his chin to check his beard from each angle, he moved on. He wasn't shaving. He didn't care.

Shuffling into the bedroom, he unzipped his bag and glanced at the clothes he'd taken off and dropped in the floor before slipping between the sheets naked at four in the morning. It was almost seven and Matt hoped the gift shop in the lobby opened soon. He'd need a clean shirt for his suit if he was to have anything to wear to his official debriefing.

He pulled his suit out of the hanging bag and tossed it on the bed. It was a little wrinkled, but not bad—at least not so bad he was concerned. After all, wrinkled seemed to be his signature fashion mark.

Digging through his dopp kit, Matt looked for a toothbrush when a heavy knock came at the door.

Tightening the towel around his waist, he looked through the peephole only to find a member of the hotel staff. The porter knocked again, blatantly disregarding the *Shhhh....* sign.

Matt cracked the door.

"Room service, Mr. Matthews."

Bewilderment crossed Matt's face. "I didn't—"

The porter pushed his way past Matt, nearly rolling over his toes as he forced the service cart into the room.

"Hey, dude. What the hell?"

"Shut the door."

At once, Matt recognized the voice from Arlington Cemetery. The man was fairly tall—over six feet. Dark hair and eyes, Matt estimated him to be in his early forties. Slightly taller than Matt, he looked lean, but as he moved Matt could tell he was a rock solid mass of muscle. Still, he was a man who could blend in anytime, anywhere. "Who the hell are you?" Matt asked.

"It doesn't matter," he replied, walking to the window to pull back the curtain and peer below. "We don't have much time."

"What the hell are you talking about?"

The man hurried back to the cart and removed the plate cover. Underneath was a nine millimeter handgun. "Take it. It's clean and unregistered."

"Why do I need a gun? Tell me who you are. Why did you warn me she was coming to kill me?

He stared at Matt without saying a word.

"She's tried you know. To kill me." Matt looked away. "I don't think she could do it. She changed her mind or something. I don't know."

"Look. I can't help you again."

"You said that the last time, and this time you're showing me your face. Why?"

"Get out of town. Leave. Eighty-six the debriefing."

"How do you know all this?"

"Because once upon a time I *was* you. Your godfather helped me. He trained me. I wanted out. He got me out, but on one condition."

"That you'd do it for me," Matt replied, his voice breathless in shock.

"That I'd do it for *anyone* who wised up and wanted the hell out. There's only been two of you and neither of you wants to cooperate."

"But how could you—"

"The less I explain, the better. Just know there are some very bad people inside the United States government, but there are also some good guys. Collie was one of the good guys."

Matt nodded. "But I need to give them this," he said, holding up the small memory drive that contained his conversation with The

Instructor in Times Square. "It's the only thing I have that proves I'm not guilty of treason. It's the only thing I have that shows he's being protected. He's an informant."

"Are you *listening* to me? They're trying to *kill you*. They don't give a shit. They want you dead. When you're dead, you're one less problem to deal with."

"If *she's* been sent to kill me that means—"

Nervously, the man walked back to the window again. "Jesus, I'd always heard you were one of the smartest agents in the field."

Matt glared at him. "I was eyes and ears," he said, staring at the gun. "I wasn't—I didn't—"

"You weren't on the elimination team."

"Yeah."

"Today you need to act like you are," he said, opening the bottom of the service cart. Taking out a uniform from the Hay-Adams, he tossed it on the bed. "Put that on. When you're ready, push this back to the service elevator and down to the basement floor. You can slip out behind the building." He glanced at Matt's suitcase. "Leave everything behind."

"Where am I going?"

"You're getting lost. You're disappearing. Because if she doesn't kill you, they'll send someone who will."

"Who is she? I mean, what's her name? And I'm not leaving town. I can't. I'm in the middle of something."

"Collie said you were hard-headed."

Matt looked back to the man. "You knew him. You *really* knew him?"

He nodded. "Get dressed and get the hell out. And this time when I say I can't help you again, I'm not lying. You won't see me—at least not like this. Be careful. And I'm sorry."

"Why are you sorry?"

"Because no one ever tells you when you sign on to do this job that your life will never be yours again. I'm sorry I didn't know you sooner. I would've told you."

"No one could've talked me out of it."

He nodded. "That's what they all say."

"And?"

"And they all end up dead."

He turned and walked away from Matt.

"Wait. I need to know her name. What is her name?"

"Jane Doe."

"Her *real* name."

"That *is* her real name."

Matt hesitated. "Really. So who does that make you?" Matt asked.

"Someone who saved your ass." The man put his hand on the door and paused. He didn't turn around but left Matt with a last word of advice. "Don't forget to take the gun."

———

DRESSED IN THE Hay-Adams uniform, Matt stared at himself in the mirror. "What the hell am I doing?" It was Collie who put him into the program. Why would Collie not trust the program to allow him out safely? The informant had at least been right about one thing—she *had* come to kill him. He knew it deep in his very being. But she couldn't. When she saw him— when he confessed his love for her—she couldn't do it. She felt it just like he did, maybe not as much or as strongly, but she felt it. Matt knew it by the way she responded to his touch, to his kiss. They'd shared something in Atlanta. She'd saved his life for a reason. She didn't have to, and yet she had. She'd come to kill him last night, and yet she didn't. She, like him, was a part of the whole. She'd signed on to be a fragment of something bigger—a greater cause than her own life. He admired and cared for her all the more. Now if he could only convince her they were playing for the same team.

At seven-thirty, Matt Matthews left room three thirteen of the Hay-Adams, pushing an empty meal service cart and wearing a hotel uniform over a pair of gym shorts and a plain white t-shirt. In the room he'd left everything he'd brought with him, including his phone and the keys to his BMW. He did take with him a hundred-dollar bill and the nine millimeter Glock, both of which he shoved so far into his jockey shorts he walked with a slightly odd gate. His biggest fear wasn't that he'd be seen by someone from Coywolf, but that he'd make a wrong move and shoot his own dick off and die in the service elevator.

Matt punched the down button repeatedly as if it would make the elevator appear faster. He was jittery. Anxious. He wasn't a covert ops guy; he was an infiltrator—a listener.

The door opened and a maid pushed her bulky cart off, not giving Matt a second thought. He jumped on board, pressing B, then prayed the elevator wouldn't stop on every floor in between.

As the doors began to close, the maid stuck her arm in stopping it. "Wait!"

Matt stepped back, grabbing his crotch in anticipation of digging out the gun.

"You forgot your cart," she said, shoving it into the now fully open doors. "Don't leave it on the floor. I'll only have to call down for you to pick it up."

Matt nodded, taking his hands off his crotch. He looked down as if he was embarrassed. He was. "Sorry."

The elevator closed and he let out a sigh of relief. Matt watched the floors light up above him, counting down like a rocket ship ready for takeoff. Breathing a sigh of relief, the doors opened at the basement floor. Staring at him was a group of men. All dressed in black suits, none of them looked to be hotel employees but more like Secret Service with their dark sunglasses and high and tight matching haircuts.

When Matt hesitated at the intimidating sight of the crew, one sounded off. "Are you getting off or what, buddy?"

Matt looked down, pretending to adjust something on the cart, pushing it forward and through the crowd of four men, keeping his head down.

The men boarded the elevator and as the doors closed one asked, "What floor?"

"Three," another answered. "Three thirteen."

DAY THREE | 0917 HOURS

KELLY SAT IN a booth at the diner. Waiting. Behind him in the adjacent booth sat Jane, alternately sipping on Pedialyte and orange juice.

"How much longer is this going to take? I got things to do," Jane said through the crack in the old vinyl seat.

"Keep those white cotton panties on."

"Who are you? Elvis?"

Kelly's eyes widened and he waived a finger in the air. "Charlie!"

Mary Charles Madewell was every bit of five feet eleven inches tall. She was built, as Kelly Casey once remarked, like a brick shithouse, but didn't seem to care. The breasts that had made many a man swoon only got in the way when she wanted to kick some serious ass. *Charlie*, as she preferred to be called, took plenty of grief over her last name as she truly was *made well.* Still, she let her skills as a decorated Secret Service officer do all the shit-talking to the boys. Blowing into the diner in black slacks that fit her like a glove and a tight fitting black sweater and leather jacket, she wore her jet hair in a low ponytail. Her dark eyes made her look more badass than she was. Deep down, Charlie had a soft spot and only truly put the hurt on those who were the worst kind of offenders—those who intentionally harmed the young, the weak or the innocent.

"How they hanging, Red?"

Kelly stood to hug her, then promptly sat down on his side of the booth. "It's good to see you, Charlie."

"So out with it," she barked, foregoing the usual *how've you been* rap.

"What? No small talk? No *what's going on in New York?*"

Charlie shook her head and waved her fingers into her body. "Talk to me. Whaddyagot?"

"No," Kelly said with a grin. "What can *you* tell *me?* I already gave you a shit-ton of information."

Charlie knitted her brow and leaned into the table. Jane pressed her shoulders against the back of the booth that separated them and turned her head, stretching like a cat. "We picked up a cell conversation on an unsecured line. He's meeting with someone tomorrow at a warehouse on the Potomac."

"Who?"

Charlie sat back. "I don't know."

"What was the conversation about?"

"You know as well as I do he's not stupid. This is the first slip up and quite frankly it makes me wonder."

"About?" Kelly asked.

"Whether or not it's a set up."

Kelly shook his head. "Set up for what?"

"For *whatever*. For *whomever*. You and I have been around long enough to know he's not the kind of guy who goes around talking on a cell line. And about a meeting location? Time and day?" Charlie shook her head. "It's too easy."

"Is it?"

"I think so."

"You think everything's too easy."

"You mean like you?"

"Hey, I'm cheap," Kelly replied. "But I'm

not easy."

"Au contraire, mon ami."

"Seriously, what do I have to lose?"

Charlie let out a punctuated laugh. "You mean other than your life?"

"C'mon, Charlie. You know me."

Jane rolled her eyes in the booth next door and shook her head at the cute tête-à-tête.

"I'll tell you what I know, but if anything happens—if *anything* goes down, we never talked."

"Of course." Kelly took a beat. "You know he's gonna be there. You *know* it."

"If he is, you might have a chance at a clear shot," Charlie said, sliding Kelly's mug of coffee away from him and taking a sip before stealing the napkin beneath it.

"If I do, you gonna look the other way?" Kelly asked.

Charlie pulled a pen from the pocket of her leather jacket and scribbled a time and address on the napkin before kissing it, leaving an imprint of her red lipstick. She tossed it back on the table and promptly slid out of the booth. "I don't know what you're talking about. I have a Homeland Security meeting tomorrow in New

York. I'm not in town. But maybe next time you roll through we could have dinner. That is, if you think you can handle me and Patricia both."

Kelly stared at the napkin and then looked back at his old friend with a toothy grin. With a single head nod he said everything he needed to.

"Ciao, Ginger-junk."

"See you *Next Tuesday*."

"Good one," Charlie said with a smile. She pointed to him with a wink and walked out the front door of the diner without looking back.

JANE WATCHED CHARLIE'S long legs parade across the black pavement of the parking lot through the window and made a face as she folded the same legs into her sports car and sped away. Only then did she leave her own booth. Picking up her Pedialyte and her backpack, she tossed a five-dollar bill on the table to tip the waitress. Pausing for a moment at Kelly's table, she didn't look at him when she spoke. "I hope that was worth something."

Kelly held up the napkin smeared with lipstick and slid out of the booth, tossing a tip for both of them from their earlier breakfast. "We need the laptop from my car and a plan. And *I* need some sleep," Kelly said, ushering Jane out the door.

"What in the hell *was* that? NYPD counter-terrorism tactics?" Jane asked as soon as they made it into the fresh air of the new morning.

"What are you talking about?"

Jane summoned a high-pitch baby voice. "I'm cheap, but I'm not easy."

"Are you *jealous?*"

Jane bristled. "No."

Kelly smiled and leaned down to look Jane in the face as they walked. "It *sounds* like you're jealous."

"I'm not."

"Yeah, well don't be. She's got a girlfriend."

Jane looked up to Kelly with only her eyes, and only for a split second.

"You heard right. She bats for the other team."

Jane took the opportunity to take a jab. "Did you force her hand?"

"What?" Kelly's voice raised into a near

shriek. "What do you mean?"

"You know," Jane said, hitching her shoulders. "To switch hit."

"What exactly are you saying?" Kelly's smile was now gone.

Jane shrugged.

"Are you insinuating I'm bad in bed?"

Jane looked both ways and crossed the street, leaving Kelly standing on the other side of the road, hands in his pockets, his ego on the street corner. "Answer me!" he shouted over the traffic now whizzing between them as they stood on opposite sides.

Jane turned to face him. The rugged cop suddenly looked like a lost child. She'd obviously hurt his feelings and now wasn't the time to play games with his heart or his pride. Besides, Jane thought Kelly was great in bed—amazing, in fact. But there was no reason to tell him—not yet anyway.

Jane shook her head *no*. "Come the hell on. We have work to do."

Kelly ran across the street before the light changed, dodging traffic to the sound of car horns blaring. Jane waited for him and when he hit the street corner, he stopped and turned to her. Grabbing her around the waist with one arm, Kelly picked her up off the sidewalk with ease and stared straight into her eyes a full three, long seconds. Then, unapologetically, he kissed her. His open mouth captured hers and Jane recoiled, remaining stiff at first. When Kelly's tongue slipped past her lips to caress the inside of her mouth, her resistance began to waiver.

Jane didn't like being taken off guard in any situation. Even this. Even a kiss. But the warmth of his lips and the feeling of security in his arms overcame her in an instant and she gave into it like sand giving way to the ocean tide. Melding into his arms, she kissed him back. It was a tango, a give and take. Kelly wrapped his other arm around her, his mouth moving down her jaw, trailing soft kisses along her long neck. When he brought his face back to her, Jane kissed *him*, parting his lips with *her* tongue. Taking command again, Kelly kissed her deeply, soulfully, over and over.

When a homeless man pushing a grocery cart full of bags and cans stopped to applaud, Jane pulled away. Neither was embarrassed, the heat between the two palpable as the ragtag man shouted, "Bravo!" Kelly took her by the hand and rushed them both into the Jambo.

Up the stairs they dashed, stopping only to laugh when Kelly tripped. Jane fumbled with the key to the room until he took it from her in frustration and unlocked the door. They hadn't spoken a word.

Slamming the door behind them, Kelly locked and leaned against it. A smile slowly inched its way across his lips.

Jane backed away from him, taking one deliberate step at a time.

"Where ya goin'?"

Jane dropped her backpack to the floor and leaned against the unmade bed. "Nowhere."

"Good." Kelly walked to her without dropping his gaze. "I've waited a lifetime to find you, Jane Doe. I'm not letting you get away now."

DAY THREE | 0930 HOURS

D R. PETER HUDSON poured himself a cup of coffee and sat at the desk in his underground lab at Max HQ. At the age of fifty-seven he'd had many accomplishments and over one thousand patents, most of which did not belong to Maxtronix Global. One that did was Ava. The Automated Voice Activated software he'd written long ago that not only dictated voice to text, but also recorded and stored memories and preferences. It was artificial intelligence that was crucial and now in the testing fields of the military to help understand the inner workings of the mind of a soldier based on the recording of not only their use of electronics, but also the tracking of their daily habits, blood pressure, heart rate, and sleep patterns. It was also used throughout the Maxtronix offices and all of Christopher

Matthews' personal homes. It was a noninvasive Big Brother, watching every move and Peter Hudson had written himself a backdoor into every user of the software platform—including the tightly firewalled Christopher Matthews' offices and homes.

Up all night cross-referencing the missing drones with at least the first few numbers of each of them mentioned in an exchange, he'd stumbled upon millions of conversations inside the software system storage. When he added the parameter of Chris Matthews, he narrowed it considerably until finally he'd latched onto each and every phone conversation Chris had where he handed over the final four digits for the drones delivered. As the drones were usually sold in pairs the conversations were spread out over the course of two years and, oddly enough, also contained information about family, sons, golf games and the weather.

Peter furrowed his brow as he carefully wrote down the information from Ava, double and triple checking to ensure he had the code sequence and drone serial number correctly logged. One false move and he and Matt wouldn't be self-destructing the drones, but instead tipping their hand to whomever had the weapons that something was amiss.

He rubbed his tired eyes and took a long swallow of his black coffee. The security door buzzed and Matteo Caruso walked in looking fresh from a good night's rest. Tall and dark, his English was perfect as he was born in the States—but so was his Italian.

"Ti sembra la merda."

Peter finally looked away from the sheet he'd studied over and over. He'd counted the sets of numbers several times. They were all there. The drones only needed to be geo-located for a safe self-destruction and they could begin. "Thank you, Matteo. I so appreciate hearing I look like shit from the man who got eight hours of sleep in our comfortable bed last night, showered in our newly remod-eled bathroom, and cuddled with our dogs this morning over Cheerios while I'm still wearing the same shirt I wore to dinner last night."

Matteo shrugged and leaned in to kiss Peter on the cheek. He and Peter had been together for fifteen years, lived together for thirteen and been married for twelve. Matteo was six one with a body like Adonis and a deep and inviting voice. Thirteen years younger than Peter, their differences never seemed to matter. Their love had no boundaries. "Come stai amore mio?"

As much as Peter loved Matteo speaking to him in Italian, this morning everything sounded like noise. "I'm done. I'm tired and I'm done," Peter proclaimed, leaning back in the chair to place his hands behind his head and stretch.

"I saw your boy this morning," Matteo said, stealing Peter's coffee for a sip. "He looks terrible if you ask me."

Peter stood. "Where?"

"Just now? Going to his private office. Sembrava merde," Matteo said gesturing with his hands. "He looks like you. Like shit."

"We're all going to hell in a handbasket, sweetheart," Peter said, pushing past his own Matteo in the lab to find the other Matthew Matthews.

Three security layers and an elevator ride later, Peter let himself into Matt's office. He could hear the sound of the shower in the adjacent washroom and decided to sit and wait it out. Peter didn't want to be seen running around the executive floor in a panic. Besides, if Matteo was correct and Matt really did look like shit when he arrived, there would be enough chatter to contain later already.

When the water shut off, Peter went to the bathroom door and knocked. "Matt? It's me. Peter."

"Come in."

Peter hesitated, then opened the door. "Ah…good—morning." He stopped in his tracks when he realized Matt was standing naked in the bathroom, still drying off his wet body with a towel.

"Yes?"

Peter found other places to put his eyes besides Matt's body. "How are you?"

Matt buffed his hair, exposing his bare and glistening physique. "Fine."

Peter looked down to his shoes. "Why don't you get dressed and meet me for *coffee*?"

Refusing to wrap the towel around his waist, Matt dug through the hotel uniform on the floor looking for a pen. Taking a thick paper guest towel that lay beside the sink, he wrote in big letters, I DON'T HAVE ANY CLOTHES. Then Matt shook his head and placed a single finger over his lips, indicating he wouldn't say anything more inside the walls of his office where his father could be listening.

Peter nodded. "I have some items I need you to look over. The house you wanted to see?"

Matt's face went blank and Peter urged him to play along. "Yes," Matt agreed wholeheartedly. "The *property*. Sure. I'll wait here."

"I'll send someone along with the, ah…information."

Matt nodded. "Great."

A LOUD RAP sounded out in Matt's office. "It's Stacy."

Matt unlocked and stood behind the door in his boxers and a towel, allowing his new secretary to enter into the large and still empty executive office.

"Oh Jesus," Stacy said, handing over a brown bag and covering her eyes. "Dr. Hudson asked me to bring these clothes and this file," she said holding each in a different hand. "I didn't know you weren't—you know—*decent*."

Matt took the file folder and tossed it on his desk. "Thanks. I've been waiting for this."

Dropping his towel as he walked toward the bathroom, Matt opened the bag and found a pair of khakis and a pink and white striped button down. Smiling wickedly at Stacy through the open door of his bathroom, he inspected the clothes. "I'm sorry. It's just that I'm not modest and I'm kind of in a hurry this morning. If we're going to work together, Stacy, you should know that I'm inappropriate as all get out. Not in a sexual way—more like an annoying little brother sort of way."

"It's okay," Stacy stammered. "I mean, I understand. I have a little brother who tried to disgust me all the time. I get it." Stacy kept her eyes on the wall opposite of the bathroom.

Really?" Matt whined, holding up the shirt Peter had sent up for him. "The *only* shirt in his closet on the premises was *pink?*"

"I'm supposed to tell you that beggars can't be choosers."

"Please tell Dr. Hudson I said thank you for the clothes and I'm glad we are close to the same size—although," Matt said with a grunt. "These khakis are a little snug."

"Is that all, sir?"

"Nope," Matt said, throwing open the door

to the bathroom completely and walking toward her, stopping only to slide his bare feet into his loafers. "Thank *you* Stacy for being a good sport this morning. Call Dr. Hudson and tell him I'm on my way."

"Done."

Matt followed Stacy out the door of his office and down the long hallway to the elevator. They parted ways when Matt took the stairwell that led to the secret entrance of the laboratory.

Matt hurried down the steps and through the security process. He was anxious to see what Peter had found, especially in light of his late night rendezvous in the woods and his early morning meeting in his hotel room. Barging into Peter's quarters, he clapped his hands together and rubbed them in anticipation. "Whatcha got?"

"Dear God," Peter gasped, now looking at him fully clothed and in the light. "You *do* look like shit."

Matt knitted his brow. "Gee thanks. I guess this is what you look like when everyone is trying to kill you, *Peter.*"

"What?"

"Never mind. Just tell me what you've got."

"A lot, actually."

"I'm all ears."

The backdoor I wrote into Ava's software worked. I won't bore you with all the geeky details—"

"Thank Jesus."

"Here's the short version: I have the codes we need."

Matt relaxed his shoulders for the first time in what seemed like two years. "Thank the Lord. So we can start destroying them."

"Well it's not quite that easy," Peter said. We have to find their precise location. I don't want to self-destruct if these crazies are storing one in a school house, and we both know that's the kind of place they'd put one. We have to be smart. If they deploy it, we can immediately self-destruct it, or if it's sitting in a cave somewhere we can also, you know, blow it there."

Matt took a deep and cleansing breath. "Good. Excellent news. You're a genius Peter. Really."

Peter shrugged and bobbed his head. "I try. It's nice to have a pat on the back from someone with the last name Matthews. That hasn't happened since your grandfather died."

Matt looked to his feet. "I'm sorry about that, Peter. I don't know why you've stuck it out this long, but I'm grateful you have. You're a true American hero, even if no one knows it."

"Well," he said, placing a hand on Matt's shoulder and giving him a wink. "Aren't those the real heroes anyway? The people no one ever knows about?"

Matt pressed his lips together and nodded. "What else did you find?"

"Ah!" Peter's eyes twinkled and he held up a finger. It was the look of a mad scientist upon discovery. "A phone conversation between your father and a nameless man. Would you like to hear it?"

"You're *this* excited about it? Hell, yeah. Play it."

Peter pressed the return key on his computer and the message recorded by Ava started to play as she began with the number the call came from, day and time. Matt made a mental note.

Yesterday, eleven a.m.
We need to meet, my old friend.

Name the time and place and I will be there. My son has come home, so I've been out of the office and working remotely. Things have settled down now.

Sons can be a blessing if they are taught well. They can also be a curse, but as I said, I want a meeting with you. I have an associate with me in Washington and we are doing some … business. Can we meet?

Yes, of course. Are you interested in buying?

Not over the phone, my friend. Not now.

I'm a busy man. I need to know it will be worth my time.

It will be worth your time.

I'm listening.

Day after tomorrow. The empty warehouse in Old Town Alexandria on the Potomac.

I know the place.

Ten in the morning.

Okay.

Matt batted his eyes in amazement. "How did we ever get *that* lucky?"

Peter shrugged his shoulders.

"This is our chance, Peter. I want to use the nanodrones. I want to take him out. We won't get another chance like this. I'm going in."

"Wait just a minute, Matt. You can't simply unilaterally decide you're going to take down a terrorist all on your own. It doesn't work like that."

Matt screwed his face into a tight ball of bewilderment and shrugged his shoulders. "What do you mean? Of *course* I can. You don't know what I've been through in the past two years, Peter. What I've witnessed to get here today? In the last two weeks I've been beaten, tied to a chair, played Russian roulette, chased, framed for treason—I'm done. Peter, listen to me. You don't have to have any part in this— really, you don't. But, no matter what you say, I'm doing this. I'm taking him out. We're blowing the drones my dad sold and I'm making things right again—if it's the last thing I do."

Peter sighed. "That's what I'm worried about Matthew. It may very well be the last thing you do and I don't know if I can live with that on my conscience."

Matt squared Peter's shoulders to meet him. He stared him in the face. "This isn't your fight. This isn't your decision. I'm doing this. Now are you going to help me or not?"

Peter stared back at him. Finally, he nodded.

"Good," Matt said, walking away. "I didn't

want to have to shoot you."

"What?"

Matt turned around and smiled. "C'mon, you knew you were gonna follow orders. I mean it's not your company. At least not yet."

Matt pushed his way through the double doors that led into another lab. He poured himself a cup of coffee and watched Peter leave for the confines of the main office.

Finally alone, Matt picked up the phone. Dialing the number he'd memorized from the recording, he waited and prayed the number was still good.

"Yes."

"It's me. Matt Matthews. We need to meet."

"We've said everything we need to say, young Matthews. Haven't we?"

"Look, Siad you can cut the bullshit. I know you have a meeting planned with my father tomorrow at ten. I'm calling to tell you he won't be running the business much longer. If you want more of the same, you're going to have to deal with me. Not to mention, he's been holding out on you, *old friend.* He's selling antiquated technology. But I'm willing to sell you the good stuff. How about we meet tomorrow at nine-thirty? Same place. You can deal with my father after."

Silence filled the airwaves and a bead of perspiration formed on Matt's forehead.

"I never took you for a man who'd betray his father. I guess I was wrong."

"Do you want to deal with the old dog or the new one? It's as simple as that."

"I'll see you at nine-thirty, young Matthews. Don't be late. And don't disappoint me."

Matt hung up and took a deep breath. Immediately he picked up the phone for call number two. Dialing, he looked through the windows of the door, making sure he was still alone.

The line rang, and Matt waited patiently for his college roommate, trusted friend and personal attorney Aldis Cantor.

"Aldis, how are you?"

"Jesus Matt, you're not calling me from jail are you?"

Matt belly laughed with his friend, and for the first time in a long time, he felt good. "No. Not in jail. I need you to change some things in my will and trust fund. How fast can you make that happen?"

DAY THREE | 1300 HOURS

JANE BATTED HER eyes open. For the first time in as long as she could remember she'd slept—hard. Lying on top of Kelly, she felt the rise and fall of his chest with each breath he took. His arm was wrapped around her perfectly shaped bottom. She traced the lines of Saint Michael up and down his muscles, delicately drifting from line to line as she silently recited the prayer to herself. Rousing Kelly from his deep slumber with her touch, his red and blond eyelashes parted revealing his bright blues. Kelly's eyes were a near perfect match to Jane's.

"How long you been awake?" he whispered, dropping a soft kiss to the top of her head.

"Not long."

Kelly rubbed his face and beard, disrupting

Jane's imaginary finger painting on his bicep. "What time is it?

"I don't know."

Kelly stretched, turning his naked and muscular body into her to meet her face head on. Stroking her cheek with the back of his fingers, he smiled at her and blinked through a satisfied and hooded gaze.

Jane took him in—every last inch. He continually surprised her—a task that was monumental to say the least. Jane wasn't one to have emotions or *feelings*—especially about men. That was part of the *more* category she never got into. That *more* place she never went to. Whenever a man wanted *more*, Jane knew it was time to cut bait. Now she found herself in an awkward place. Jane wanted *more* from Kelly Casey.

"Tell me about your dad."

A gentle smile broke out, not just across his lips, but his entire face. It was obvious Kelly Casey loved and respected his father. "What do you want to know?"

"Everything."

"He was an amazing man." Kelly rolled onto his back and stared at the ceiling, pulling

Jane close to him. In turn she threw her leg over his torso, his heavy manhood resting under her leg. "He loved my mother *so* much. They were inseparable. He always said from the moment he met her, he knew he was going to marry her. It was love at first sight."

"You think that really happens?"

Kelly looked down at her and narrowed his gaze before kissing her sweetly on the lips. "Of course it does."

"My father was just home from the service and my mom was working at a bakery. One of the other girls she worked with was a newlywed. She'd married Dad's older brother and told my mom she wanted to fix her up with her new brother-in-law. I guess Mom balked at first, but then finally said yes. He took her to a high school football game—you know that's a big deal in Pittsburgh on a Friday night. Anyway, it was cold and he gave her his coat. She stayed warm and he froze to death. He knew he loved her and she knew he'd always take care of her—and he did."

Jane squeezed her eyes shut. "That's quite a story."

"Mmmhmm. You want to hear another

one?"

"Sure."

"One night my dad found a baby in a dumpster. Baby Doe. And because he could never solve the murder case of the woman he *knew* was her mother—although no one would allow him to put her in the police report—he carried that report with him until the day he died. He looked for Baby Doe his *whole* life because he felt responsible for her. And when he died, he asked me to do the same."

Jane's eyes flooded with tears—tears she couldn't hold back. "I guess I just don't understand," she said, choking on her emotion. "Why would someone care about a baby that no one wanted? I mean, it didn't affect him. He was going home to his own wife—his *own* baby."

Kelly pulled away to look her in the face. Jane quickly wiped the tears from her eyes. "Are you serious?" he asked.

Jane said nothing.

"Jane, *someone* wanted you. Your *mother* wanted you."

"How could you know that?"

"Because she didn't get an abortion. The

file clearly shows she reported a sexual assault nine months before. She would've had every reason to do it." Kelly sat up in bed, taking Jane with him. Tucking the sheet under her arms, she sat cross-legged staring at him. Her face splotchy with emotion, Jane was the most vulnerable she'd been in twenty years. "Jane, you were loved whether you knew it or not."

Tears uncontrollably filled her eyes again. "Stop saying that."

"It's true. What my dad did? That was love, Jane. He never stopped looking for you. He never stopped worrying about you. He remembered you every year on your birthday."

Jane climbed out of bed taking the sheet with her, leaving Kelly naked and alone. "Stop it!" she shouted. "Stop saying these things to me."

"Stop what? Stop telling you the truth?"

Out of bed, Kelly wrapped his arms around Jane, pulling her in as she began to sob. "Let it out, baby. Let it all out."

"Don't tell me he cared."

"I'm sorry. I *have* to. He did. He cared *so much*. He worried about you. He wondered where you were, if you were alive. He stopped kids on the street all the time, looking for you."

"Really?" Jane sniffed. "Why?"

"Because I think somehow he knew deep down, you needed him."

Jane began to softly cry. Kelly held her even tighter. "And now, he said kissing the top of her head. "Now, I know you need *me*." Jane stopped and looked up to him. He brushed her new blonde locks from her eyes and gently kissed her lips. "And *I* need you."

DAY THREE | 1500 HOURS

"GIVE IT TO me straight without a lot of technical mumbo jumbo, Peter. You know I'm not that smart, nor am I in the mood to feel even more inadequate than I already do."

Standing in the Mia V testing room, Peter rolled his eyes. "It's not rocket science, Matthew."

"No, Peter. It's Micro Insect Air Vehicle Science and it's above my paygrade."

"Let's not get dramatic."

"You know what I mean. What's our plan of attack? I need to know what I'm walking into."

"We can do it a couple of different ways," Peter replied.

"I'm listening."

"I can use the camera—"

Matt blanched. "Are you fucking kidding

me right now? There's a camera in that tiny little mosquito head?"

Peter tilted his head slightly and raised his brows. "You've been in the desert a while Matt. Of course there's a camera. Or we can use a heat-seeking locator."

Matt crossed his arms. "I'm listening."

"It's a tiny adhesive patch. You place it on one of your fingers, touch the target and you've essentially painted them. It heats up just slightly more than normal body temperature, the Mia V knows it's a target, takes aim and—"

"Pop goes the weasel," Matt added.

"So to speak."

"So option one, you get a front row seat. Option two there's less room for error."

Peter shook his head. "No. There's no room for error with either one."

"How do the Mia V's get into the target zone?"

"We can deploy a few tactics, but it would be easiest if you took them into the kill zone yourself."

Matt nodded. "And how do I do that?"

"Have you ever eaten a breath mint from a tin box before?" Peter asked.

"Of course. Who hasn't?"

"Exactly."

"You will have the Mia V's in a small metal tin. When you get into the target location, you'll open the box like you are getting yourself a mint and release the drones. Then paint the target and step away from the kill zone. They'll do the rest."

"How many drones are you sending me in with?"

"How many do you want?"

"I don't know Peter. How many will I need to take this man down? I don't want to be stuck in a warehouse with a terrorist and the only weapon I have is an ass-kicking mosquito the size of my fingernail."

Peter's stoic expression said he was not amused with Matt's assessment of the scenario. "You'll need one drone, Matthew. If you do your job correctly, you'll need one."

Without hesitating, Matt made his final request. "I want four drones and two targets. Just in case."

"Done."

DAY THREE | 1600 HOURS

"KEEP THE CHANGE." Kelly handed the delivery kid who didn't look a day over thirteen a twenty-dollar tip. "And stay out of trouble, you hear?"

"Wow. Thank you, sir. I will."

Kelly stood at the doorway of the room in just his jeans and nothing else. Jane hid in the bathroom when the knock came at the door, slipping on her underwear and pulling a sweatshirt over her head. They'd stayed in bed all day. Jane crying off and on. Kelly making love to her off and on. It was four o'clock in the afternoon. He was famished and dehydrated. She was mentally and physically exhausted.

"Come on, baby," Kelly said, hitching up his jeans with one hand and balancing the pizza, a mound of napkins and four bottles of water stacked on top. "You need food."

"Don't you mean *you* need food?" she replied, climbing back on the bed to straighten the quilt over the mussed sheets. There was only one chair in the small room, and the desk was covered in the police file—something Jane didn't want to disturb. The bed was their only place to eat.

Jane took the water bottles from atop the box and Kelly tossed it between them as he sat, wasting no time to flip open the pizza box and promptly fold a slice into his mouth for a bite.

"Geez Casey."

"Sorry," he mumbled, his mouth still full from his first mammoth bite. Rolling his eyes back in his head he moaned. "All that lovemaking made me crazy-hungry."

"You mean sex," Jane corrected, not looking at him as she took a piece.

Kelly dropped the pizza slice and licked the grease from his finger before opening one of the bottles of water to take a long drink. He stared at Jane without dropping his gaze. "I've had plenty of things that belong to you in my mouth today and I've loved every moment of it, but don't put your words in my mouth, Jane. I know what I said, and I know exactly what I meant."

Jane said nothing. Instead she took a small bite of pizza and dropped her chin to her chest, bringing only her eyes up to see if he was still watching her. He was.

Kelly Casey grinned at Jane and she cracked a smile. Then he let out a deep sigh. "We need a plan, Jane."

She nodded. "I know."

Dropping the pizza slice, she wiped her hands on a napkin and walked over to the desk, gathering up the papers from the file and the lipstick stained napkin from Charlie's visit at the diner.

Sitting cross-legged, Jane began to sort through every paper in the file, setting the evidence she didn't care to see, like photographs from the scene of her mother's murder to the side. "Now that I can think rationally about this, walk me through the crime scene. Everything you know."

"Dorothy Odessa Ellison. Born September, 15, 1966. She was twenty-one when she died. No living relatives."

"What?" Jane shuffled through papers. Kelly was giving the information from rote.

"Nope," he said, tossing another piece of crust into the box. "Her parents died while she was in college. Car accident. She didn't have any living relatives."

"She was an orphan," Jane whispered, staring at the photograph of her mother she'd placed at the top of the bed.

"Siad was born in the U.S. His mother and father were here, studying in New England. His father worked for the government—it's pretty sketchy what he might have done—his mom stayed at home. When he was ten, they moved back to the Middle East. It gets sketchy again but pretty widely held that during those eight years he was radicalized. He came back to the United States in 1984 for college."

"At Pitt. Where he met my mother." But why all the secrecy? Why couldn't your father nail him?"

"He couldn't prove anything. I mean he was a beat cop, but he said he thought Siad's father had protection—immunity from the government."

"Your dad was correct," Jane replied. "His father was an informant—an *important* one. Then he wasn't. And then he was dead."

"So the old man was right. Wow. Dad thought he was a spy. Said he couldn't risk having his kid in the limelight of a murder trial. It was all swept under the rug. Everything. Including your mother. Including you."

Jane laid flat on the bed and stared at the ceiling. "I'm sorry I never got to meet your father. He sounds like a smart man. A great cop."

"He was the best," Kelly agreed. "And you *did* meet him."

Jane sat up. "Okay. What else?"

Kelly pulled the official college transcripts of Dessa Ellison from the pile. "She was intelligent. School of Engineering, she had a grade point average of three point nine," Kelly said. "Smart cookie."

Jane sat back into her hips and dropped her shoulders. "Dammit. She was going to be an engineer."

Kelly nodded. "Here's your real birth certificate—I mean in case you've not seen it."

Jane slid off the bed and walked to where she'd dropped her backpack hours earlier. Digging inside, she took out the small tin wrapped in a rubber band. Gripping the Sucrets box, rusty at the hinges, she placed in on the bed and crawled back on.

Kelly glanced at it and back to Jane. Then closing the pizza box, he tossed it on the floor. "What's this?"

Jane gave him a tiny shrug of her shoulders. She'd been more open and honest with Kelly Casey than anyone in her entire life. He knew more about her in a few short days than anyone ever had. There was no turning back now. "This is everything."

He picked it up, his fingers running over the worn off lettering. "What do you mean, *everything?*"

"I've been tossed from place to place my whole life. I don't know anything else. Most of my worldly possessions have always fit inside either a garbage bag or that backpack. This," she said taking the tin box from him. "This contains everything that has meaning to me. Or is supposed to."

Kelly stroked her arm, giving it a doting squeeze. "I'm not following, baby. What do you mean *supposed* to?"

Jane's eyes twitched at the way he affectionately referred to her as *baby*. It was thoughtful, sincere and loving. She didn't know what to do with it, so she ignored it. "I—I mean," she stumbled through her words and thoughts. "It's just, there are things in here that sort of *came* with me. I don't know what they mean, but they're mine all the same. I guess I always thought someday I'd understand it better."

Jane kept her eyes down. Kelly dropped his face to meet them. "Do you want to share them with me? It's okay if you don't."

"No," she whispered. "I think you're the only one who might be able to help me understand some of it."

"Okay," he said, sitting up.

Jane unwrapped the tight rubber band and set it aside as was her usual ritual with the box. This time instead of laying out the pieces of her life to display them like fragments of evidence in a mystery, Jane kept each piece inside the tin. She was ready to treat herself with compassion, and these tiny bits of history were a testimony to the fact that she was alive with thought and feeling. Regardless of the path she'd had to this point and those who'd treated her as though she was less than human, she'd come to a fork in the road. *Her* road.

Jane picked up the first photo. "This is Havis Mansoor. She was the first person to ever care about me."

"Actually," Kelly corrected. "She's the third. My parents were first."

Jane looked into Kelly's blue eyes and nodded. "I stand corrected. She's the *third* person to ever care about me. She was my first caseworker. She was killed in Pittsburgh at the community center during the terror attack. She was a volunteer."

"Jesus. Not the one…"

"Yes. The same attack that killed ninety and injured a hundred. The same attack that was planned by *him*."

Kelly sighed. Jane moved on to the next item. Another photo. "This is Jen. Jennifer Drenkowski. She was the first real girlfriend I ever had—first one I ever trusted." Jane smiled as she handed the small photo over.

"You look alike," Kelly remarked. "Well, except for the blonde hair you've got going on now."

Jane nodded. "We have the same initials too. It was kind of a running joke—Jen and

Jane. But when a bounty went out on my head for killing two of Siad's senior men, she was captured, raped and beheaded. They tortured her and filmed every moment of it." Jane looked away. "It was supposed to be me."

Kelly filled his lungs with air, but didn't exhale. Finally, he said only her name. "*Jane.*"

She ignored him and moved on. "I've always had this," she said holding up the diaper pin with the pink head. "I don't even know if it's mine. I always fantasized that someone cared enough to dress me like a little girl with a bow in my hair and a pink dress and on my diaper were two pink diaper pins." Jane told her made up fairytale and gazed at the pin, now starting to fall apart. "It's just a stupid story I tell myself, but…"

Kelly took it from her. "It's not. You know why I know?"

Jane looked back to him.

"Because I had the blue version of these in my baby book. My mom was quite the environmentalist and didn't believe in disposable diapers. I never wore them. If you were at my house, and I know you were, you wore cloth diapers. My mom did this, and I can promise you, she did it with love—because she did everything with love." he said handing it back to her. "I'd bet my life on it."

Jane took it back and gripped in in her hand. It was as if she'd willed something good from the tiny scrap of her life and it had come true.

"What else do you have?"

Jane took a deep breath and picked up the red ribbon and shook her head. "I have absolutely no idea what this is."

A huge smile crossed Kelly's face. Taking the red ribbon from her hand he dropped his head back in laughter. "Oh my gosh, *Mom*," he whined.

"What?"

"It's an old Irish tradition. Mothers tie a red string or a red ribbon to their baby's crib until their first birthday. It's supposed to ward off the fae. *The fairies.*"

"I don't—"

Kelly started laughing again. "Irish moms are superstitious—well, the Irish are just superstitious in general but—oh my God, she wanted to protect you." Covering his mouth with his hand he paused. It was clear to Jane that Kelly's mother was an extraordinary woman. They were a family who loved and cared for each other deeply.

Kelly handed the string back to Jane. "You've got some really good stuff here," he said with a smile. "I mean, you've been carrying around meaningful things, Jane."

"Yeah," she replied. "I mean, I guess."

"Keep going," he said, "This is getting good."

Jane took the silver sixpence from the tin and placed it in Kelly's open palm. He nodded.

"Are you going to tell me you know what this is too?"

Kelly stood from the bed and walked to the desk by the door. Moving his badge and wallet aside, he sorted through the loose change he'd tossed out earlier when he'd picked his pants up off the floor after Jane removed them in a frantic rush. Walking back to Jane, he held in the air, a coin. He tossed it to her as he laid down on his side, propping his head up and smiling. Jane caught it overhanded. Opening her grip, she smiled.

"Sometimes Irish parents put a silver coin in their baby's hand to hold during the

Christening. It's for a prosperous life."

Jane held the two up together. Kelly's was worn from where he'd plainly been carrying it around with him for most of his adult life. "Are you telling me that—" Jane stopped herself.

Kelly smiled. "I'm saying it's too obvious to just be a coincidence. I think my parents, even though they were forced to hand you over, wanted to protect you as much as they could.

She unfolded the police report. It had been redacted to the point there was nothing to see, only the date of her birthday, her name, Baby Doe and the last three numbers in Kelly's father's badge. She handed it to him and he looked at it for only a moment. Then as he was just about to hand it back, did a double-take. A look of surprise came over him. "His badge number."

Jane said nothing.

"That's how you figured it out."

"That and your story."

Kelly cocked his head. "One truth, one wish, one lie?"

Jane nodded. "Your father's unsolved case."

Kelly's eyes brightened. It was apparent he

understood.

"You said it was nearly thirty years old, like me. Unsolved, also like me. And happened in Pittsburgh."

Their first night together, Kelly had asked her to play a game—a game in which he wanted to find out more about her. She was to tell him three stories—one had to be true, another a lie, another a wish. Kelly told the story of his father's unsolved case. Jane knew it was his truth. Jane told a story of breaking a dish and being punished—dragged into the snow barefoot and in her pajamas as a tiny girl. Kelly had thought it a wild tale and obviously a lie.

Kelly sat back on the bed, looked away and came back to her unwavering gaze. "The story about being chained to a dog house. That was true?"

Jane bit her lip and looked away. Even now, she didn't want to admit her *truth*.

"In the snow? Barefoot?"

She nodded.

Kelly pulled Jane from the bed to stand with him. Wrapping his arms around her he tucked her head into his chest with his massive hand and hugged her tightly. Rocking her back and forth, he kissed her on the head and said, "Whatever you want to do, I'm with you. One hundred percent. No matter what. And I promise you, you'll never be alone like that again, because I will always have your back."

Taking Jane by the shoulders he placed her at arms-length to look her in the face. "We know where he'll be tomorrow. Let's go get the motherfucker."

Jane nodded.

"Is there anything else in your little box?"

"A cigarette. Marlboro."

Kelly recoiled.

"I'll smoke it when he's dead."

DAY FOUR | 0300 HOURS

MATT SAT ON a plush couch in a lounge room inside Peter's hidden lab at Maxtronix, his hands folded in contemplation, or perhaps prayer. It was all the same to him tonight. With nowhere to go and their plan only a few hours away, sleep wasn't in his future anyway. On the coffee table in front of him was a small briefcase containing the Mia V mosquitos. Each filled with the maximum dosage of tetrodotoxin, the tiny flying drones contained enough toxins to take down one hundred and twenty men. Matt only needed to take down two. The small heat patches the drones would use as targets were conveniently placed on a plastic sheet in the shape of a hand. Peter took the guesswork out of everything in the event Matt was feeling twitchy. All he had to do was match his own hand to the one on the table. The patches would adhere to his fingertips. As long as Matt didn't inadvertently touch the wrong person, the plan would go off without a hitch.

Next to the killer drones were the legal documents Aldis Cantor had dropped everything to draw up. It was only a backup, but it needed to be done. Matt knew he was walking into a shit show where anything was likely to happen. Because of that, he needed to be prepared for any outcome.

There was a letter and computer USB drive for Peter, a letter for his father, and a letter and a USB drive for her. Finally, he'd left an envelope with Peter to be mailed *only* in the event of his death. With nothing but a P.O. Box listed as an address, it was his back-up plan—his confession to a fellow reporter he trusted. He'd had a difficult time convincing Peter to accept the final task not knowing what it was or to whom it was being sent. It was almost as difficult convincing Aldis of what he'd wanted done—fighting *him* tooth and nail the entire day—but once it was completed, it was finished and Matt was satisfied.

Earlier he'd signed the documents one by

one in front of Stacy, who notarized every last page, making it all legally binding. Then, Matt made a quick video of himself to insure his sound and stable state of mind should anyone decide to question it.

Finally stretching out on the couch, he tucked his hands behind his head and closed his eyes, thinking of the time he'd shared with Jane in Atlanta. A smile crossed his face when he thought of the night she asked for sex and he turned her down. He shook off his own madness. "Idiot," he said aloud. She'd saved his life and in their one night together, he knew she cared for him. He knew it the way he understood the sun would rise or the tide would change. Not because it had always been that way, but because inside he knew they were a part of something bigger he wasn't meant to understand—not yet. But he would. Someday. Matt knew just as she'd saved his life, he would mean something to Jane for the rest of hers.

With a heavy sigh, Matt Matthews settled his body into the deep contours of the soft couch. There was no turning back now.

DAY FOUR | 0600 HOURS

JANE STARED AT her backpack by the door. She'd packed everything while Kelly showered before bed. By the time *she* showered, he was out cold. Jane tried to sleep. Mostly she listened to Kelly breathe. She watched him move by the light of the moon through the cracked blinds in her window at the Jambo— the room she'd not left in over twelve hours. It was truly longer than she'd stayed in any one place in as long as she could remember—aside from staking out a kill.

Still reeling from everything she'd learned in the last few hours, she tried to stay on track, to do what she did best—eliminating numbers on *The List*. As she watched Kelly's chest rise and fall she told herself there was no way she could drag him into what she was about to undertake. Kelly operated with rules and standards. Jane was about getting the job done. And no matter what he said, and Jane felt he was being sincere, she couldn't in good faith take him under and into the dirty world in which she operated. She'd already shown him the photos of Havis and Jen. She didn't want to add his face to her box of memories, carrying him with her wherever the wind blew. It wasn't fair to Kelly and it wouldn't be fair to Jake Casey. The man had saved her life. She refused to repay him by ruining his son's career as a decorated NYPD officer. No way. Not on Jane's watch.

She wanted to kiss him but refrained, afraid it might be just enough to wake him. Instead she did something she never did. She prayed. It wasn't anything formal—more of a conversation with God—a God she thought had long forgotten about her. She said a word of thanks for explaining her life to her, asked Him to keep Kelly safe and ended with the prayer of Saint Michael.

When she was finished, she wiped the single tear she'd shed and slowly climbed out of the bed, not making a sound. Taking the police file from the desk, she stared at the address and time on the napkin once more.

Unlatching the chain, she turned the deadbolt as quietly as possible. The doorknob squeaked and Jane looked over her shoulder to see if Kelly moved. Rousing slightly from his back, he rolled over on his side, facing away from Jane. She took one last look at him then noticed his silver sixpence mixed back in with his change. Quickly she shoved her hand into her pocket, taking out her own. Setting it beside his, she moved them both away from the rest of his loose change, placing them side by side. Jane slipped out the door and closed it as silently as the old lock would allow.

Jane walked away and didn't look back. Jane never looked back.

RIDING THROUGH COLUMBIA Heights on the Harley, Jane drove toward her ultimate destination. She stopped at a scenic overlook of the Potomac River, parking the chopper in the bushes as best she could. Digging the burner phone from her bag, Jane looked at the time and knew it was early, but not too early. She had a thirty-minute window to make her call. It was now or never.

Dialing, she wondered if he'd even believe her when she said the words.

"Hello."

"Father?"

"Yes?"

"It's me."

Father Doheny sounded tired—more tired than usual. "Where are you?"

"I'm coming home."

She heard a sigh of relief on the other end. "I'm so glad. I'm *so* glad. When?"

"Tomorrow. Maybe the next day."

"Are you okay?"

"I'm...*different*. I have some things to discuss with you. I need to make some decisions."

"I'm very happy and relieved you're finished with this...with..."

Jane cut him off. "I'll see you soon."

"I'll have your *things* ready for you."

"I thought you'd tell me you didn't believe me."

"I can hear it in your voice."

"What do you hear?"

"Peace. Humanity."

Jane peeked around the corner of the bushes. It was a foggy morning and although she hadn't heard anyone, seeing them was a different story. "Let's not get carried away with ourselves, Father. Okay?"

"I'll see you soon, my child. Be safe and come home in one piece."

"Bye."

Jane turned off the phone and slipped it into her backpack. She looked to her watch. It was *go time.*

DAY FOUR | 0917 HOURS

ARRIVING AT THE address Charlie had given, Jane found herself at an abandoned area filled with warehouses. Posted with placards everywhere, it looked as if the city had taken it over for renovation and preservation, but miles of red tape had obviously taken its toll. Each year a new number was placed over the last, showing their intent to get the project rolling but also their complete inability.

Fog rolled off the Potomac and a luxury boat motored by. Jane parked the Harley fifty yards away. It was loud enough to not only be annoying, but noticeable to anyone just hanging out.

She spied the front door, but opted for a window, high above the fire escape. Climbing like a monkey, Jane made it to the second story window, throwing open the sash to climb in blind. She didn't know what was inside or below, but it was better than having her ass hanging in the wind.

Inside, she balanced on a ledge until her eyes adjusted in the darkness. She needed to assess her options. As her pupils dilated, she surveyed the entire warehouse. Open and mostly empty, it offered little coverage for a gun fight. Shipping pallets were stacked in a semi-circle approximately six feet high, leaving a clear path to the side entrance. The loading docks were closed and Jane could see large padlocks ensuring none of them could be opened. Aside from a few barrels and a pile of gravel, the warehouse was barren with the exception of what was immediately underneath her. Below were marine fenders. Large and still partially inflated PVC-coated balloons, large ships used them to keep from banging into the side of the dock. She had one option and she took it. Jumping forty feet, she landed on it ass first. The fender burst on impact as the air broke her fall. It sounded like a dying animal and quickly deflated.

The fenders made for good cover, although they wouldn't allow for protection in a gunfight and that was what this was going to be.

Today there would be no drugs, no set-ups or storylines. Jane was there to kill, devil-may-care, then get the hell out. It was the number one reason Kelly couldn't be with her.

Walking the area below, Jane decided to hunker down between a fender and a steel beam reaching high into the rafters of the warehouse. She took two guns from her backpack, locking and loading both. Jane had a Colt M1911 in her hand, a Glock in the waistband of her pants, a Bowie knife in her boot, a switchblade in her back pocket and one lethal syringe in the pocket of her hoodie.

If need be, Jane was willing to stick the syringe in her own leg. No matter what happened today, Three was not taking her life. She'd end it all herself before giving him the satisfaction.

Fully loaded, Jane did what she'd done so many times before. She waited. This time, it was personal.

When the doors opened five minutes later, they walked in. All three of them together, all three of them in dark suits and white shirts with no tie. Jane's stomach turned.

"I was surprised to hear from you," Three said to Matt. "I thought I made it clear to you that our business was finished.

"I have something I think you'll want to know. It's why I wanted to have a word with you before my father came today."

"Search him," Three said to Four.

Matt put his hands in the air, turning on command as Four patted him down from top to bottom. "I assure you, I'm only here to talk business, nothing more."

"What's this?" Four asked, grabbing at the front pocket of Matt's pants.

Matt pulled out the small tin and showed it to him. "Breath mints. Would you like one? 'Cause you need one, my friend."

Four replied. "No." Then turned to Three and spoke in Arabic to tell him Matt was clean.

Jane shook her head and watched Matt open the tin, popping a mint into his mouth, then offer the mints up a second time to Four. *Cocksuckingmotherfuckingsonofabitch.*

"What's this about?" Three asked.

"Can we speak in private?" Matt asked, gesturing slightly toward Four's presence.

"No, we cannot. Whatever you have to say,

you can say in front of the both of us."

"My father is hiding something pretty important from you."

"What?"

"Yes, Matthew." Christopher Matthews, wearing his dark suit, walked into the crowd through the rows of pallets. "What am I hiding?"

Jane flinched. A bead of sweat formed on her forehead as she looked with one watchful eye from her vantage point as the scenario unfolded.

"Let's all take a breath here," Matt said, patting his father on the back of the neck with his open palm. Then walking to Three, he did the same. "The last time I checked, we're all business associates—*friendly* business associates. I just want to make sure I'm in the know, especially since my father has been trading with you in my name."

"Son, you don't know what you're talking about."

"I know more than you think, Dad."

Three began to laugh and Four joined in. The more he smiled the more Jane wanted to pull the trigger. But she couldn't. She couldn't get a clean shot—Christopher Matthews was like a nervous mother watching her overachieving child. He paced frantically back and forth, never allowing Jane a true line of sight.

"Sons have a way of making us proud while trying to be their own leaders. I know this. I know this well. Sons are a blessing, Chris. Sons are a blessing if you can contain them, teach them and raise them to—"

"To what?" Matt asked with a laugh. "To be like you? You kill people. That's your job and it was my job to follow you and tell our military when and where you were going and what the hell you were doing. That's right, Dad. I wasn't *just a journalist.* I've been part of a national security team that's been keeping you from taking thousands of innocent lives, you piece of shit."

Three turned to Christopher. "Your son needs to learn respect."

"My son needs to learn a lot of things."

Jane listened to every word Matt said. The shock of his confession took her out of her head. She lost focus and took a step back. Dizzy with confusion, Jane shook it off mentally and physically when Four came into her view and she had a clear shot.

Taking dead aim between his eyes, she blocked out the argument rattling in the background between Matt and his father. Exhaling, she locked her sights, and squeezed the trigger, never so sure of a shot in her life.

Firing three rounds into his head, the explosive BAM! BAM! BAM! caused the men to scatter. Four dropped, one shot between the eyes, one shot through the eye socket and the final blow to the forehead. The force sent him tumbling back and to the ground.

Jane bolted from her firing spot, anticipating retaliation. Moving through the shadows, she saw the top of Christopher Matthews' head as he ducked behind a stack of pallets. He was a sitting duck, but not on her kill list—at least not today. Jane scanned the room, keeping her back against the wall. Working her way through the tight space, the area had become smaller now that she had nowhere to go.

Finding a sheltered spot behind another pile of wooden pallets, she waited, the warehouse now silent. There was only one way in and out, and Jane had it covered. It was every man for himself.

Catching a shadow, Jane knew she had two choices; she could shoot to wound and apologize later if she hit Christopher or Matt, or go for the kill and not look back. As the footsteps neared, she caressed the trigger with her index finger. She'd never been so anxious to make a move in her life.

When he stepped into view all Jane could see was a dark suit jacket. She fired one shot into the shoulder.

When he went down, she hurried out of hiding to finish the job. At her feet, writhing in pain and bleeding was the mastermind of the terror attack that killed Havis Mansoor, the man who called for the rape, torture and beheading of Jennifer Drenkowski and the man who murdered her own mother, Dessa Ellison. Jane kicked his body over then came to his head, lifting him by the shoulders and dragging him to a pile of gravel nearby.

Sitting him up, she stood back and stared, watching him bleed and gasp for air. She'd hit more than his shoulder. She'd pierced a lung.

"Look what we've got here," Jane said, pacing back and forth in front of him. "Do you know how long I've waited for this moment?

How long I've dreamed of this?" Jane asked, unable to control the sick and wicked smile on her face. Her body coursed with adrenaline, her heart raced with hate.

Three stared at her, his breathing heaving and labored.

Matt Matthews rushed to the scene, Chris on his heels. "Jane. Are you okay?"

Shocked by the sound of her own name, Jane turned, taking her attention off of Three for a split second.

Siad al Daleel ul Khyayraat reached across his waist, pulling free a Smith and Wesson revolver. He aimed for Jane and she flinched at the sight, firing off a round, hitting him in the upper chest.

Three fired in rapid succession. Jane heard only one word. "No."

Shoved aside, Jane's second shot was off target. Seemingly, without thought or fear, Matt Matthews used his body as a shield from the bullets meant for Jane as Three emptied the chamber of his revolver directly into Matt's chest cavity.

Back on her feet, Jane rushed to Matt's side. Cradling his head in her hands, he looked up at her, his eyes full of shock. "I know who you are, Jane Doe. I know who you are."

Jane nodded. "That's right. I'm Jane. Hang on, Matt. Hang on."

Matt blinked slowly. Jane could feel the warmth of his blood cover her legs as she cradled him. He was bleeding out. "I've thought about you since the moment I met you," he whispered in punctuated gasps. "You saved my life, Jane. I saved yours."

Jane nodded. "You saved my life, Matt."

"I'm not a bad guy. I'm just like you, Jane."

"You're one of the good guys, Matt. I know. I know. Why'd you have to be a hero? Why?"

Matt winced in pain, life draining from his body. Then staring into the blue of Jane's eyes he whispered. "Don't talk."

"What?" Jane shook her head. "Matt—I"

"You're still talking."

Jane took his hand and squeezed it.

"This is my accomplishment, Jane," he said with a smile. "*This.*"

Taking his final breath, Matt Matthews died in Jane's arms, his heart no longer beating, his blood covering her hands—her clothes—her guilty conscience. Jane passed her fingertips over his eyes, closing them for the final time, then looked up and into the horrified face of Matt's father, standing over his son's lifeless body.

"What have I done?" Christopher Matthews cried, falling to his knees at Matt's side.

Jane looked back at Three. Gasping for air, he held on to his empty gun. Standing, Jane walked in calculated strides toward him. Covered in Matt's blood, she kicked the gun from Three's hand, pulling her second gun from the back of her waistband.

Cocking the Glock, she shoved it under Three's chin, forcing his head back. "Look at me, you piece of shit. I want you to look at me when I say this to you."

Three turned his blue eyes to stare into hers.

"I want you to see me. Do you see me?"

Three nodded.

"On your way to hell—to *Jahannam*—I want you to remember this face." It was the speech Jane had given so many times before. This time, she could barely get the words to cross her lips. Her eyes wild with fury, her body shaking with rage. "You are dying at the hands of a woman. Do you understand? There will be no virgins for you, no beautiful welcome. You are going to burn in *Hellfire* and suffer with Shaitan for the rest of eternity." Jane shoved the gun farther into his neck and listened to him gasp. "Tell me you understand what I've just said to you. *Say it!*" She shouted into his face, as her eyes welled with tears. Spittle falling from her lips, she screamed, "Say it!"

"Baby Doe." The words were faint as blood trickled from Three's mouth. He was struggling to catch a breath. Jane didn't care. She wanted him to suffer.

"What did you say?"

"You are Baby Doe."

Jane curled her lip and gritted her teeth. "And you killed my mother."

Three began to laugh. It was soft at first, mostly because it was all he could manage with what air he had in his lungs, but it grew louder as he seemed to find strength from a place so evil, Jane couldn't fathom.

"Dessa Ellison was her name."

"I know who she was, you stupid girl."

Jane shoved the gun harder against his throat.

"She lied to me," he said.

"You killed her."

"She told me she got an abortion. But she didn't. I had to take care it myself."

Jane felt dizzy. The once sure grip she had on the gun and her reality slipped.

"It's no wonder. *Jane.*"

Jane began to come unhinged from her own existence. Her hands trembling, her heart pounding, her ears ringing.

"You're a killer. *Jane.*"

Tears streamed down her twisted face. Jane's eyes fixed on Three as she shook her head.

"*Because you're mine.*"

The words dripped from his lips as blood poured from his mouth. Taking a loud and audible breath, she backed away from him, dropping the gun she'd held so tightly under his chin to her side.

Three laughed hysterically, blood spewing from his mouth.

Jane stood immobile. A crack in the universe had caused her to break with reality.

"Jane!" Touching her on the shoulder, Kelly dashed from body to body checking to see if anyone was still alive. Jane hadn't noticed him rushing into the warehouse. "Jane, you have to get out of here. There's a fleet of squad cars on their way. Get out! Right now!"

"Run! *Woman*!" Three mocked her, coughing up blood.

Jane took two steps back to him.

"Jane, I'm serious," Kelly pleaded. "Get out of here! Don't do it. Look around you. Hasn't there been enough bloodshed for the day?"

"Don't worry," Three mumbled through his bloody spittle. "She won't kill me. She can't kill *her father*."

Jane stepped away and looked at Matt lying dead at her feet, his father in a heap crying beside him. She looked back to Kelly still wild-eyed, and exhaled. Breathing hard and full of adrenaline, Kelly nodded to her. She stepped away from the scene. Kelly walked to Matt's body and knelt down beside it. Sirens blared in the distance.

Improvise. Adapt. Overcome.

Turning without warning, Jane stared down the blue eyes that matched her own. He smiled at her, blood dripping from his evil grin. Jane lifted the Glock from her side, took aim and fired one shot, hitting Siad al Daleel ul Khyayraat between the eyes.

She watched the bullet enter his head. She witnessed the wicked sneer leave his lips. Jane waited until she saw it—the vacant and lifeless stare of a dead man.

Then Jane allowed the gun to slip from her fingers, hitting the concrete floor below her. Sirens blaring, Kelly shouted at her and frantically waved his arms. She couldn't hear him—she heard nothing but the thrum of her own heart.

Turning, Jane walked away without a single word.

She didn't look back. Jane never looked back.

DAY FOUR | 1003 HOURS

PETER HUDSON WATCHED the monitor in horror. The four drones still circling the area were sending back every camera angle. Not only had Peter watched Matt die, it had been recorded in the Maxtronix memory bank.

It was time. Peter could hear the police coming. Giving the command, drones one and two were sent to their target—Christopher Matthews.

Watching live, Chris Matthews slapped at the pinch on his neck. Target engaged. Within seconds, he collapsed. Peter cut the feed and self-destructed the remaining Mia V's when he witnessed the unknown police officer in the building.

Turing off the monitors, Dr. Peter Hudson disengaged from the system entirely. He was haggard, distraught and unbeknownst to him, he was, according to the papers left on his desk at five in the morning by Matt Matthews, the new CEO and majority shareholder in Maxtronix Global.

DAY FOUR | 1103 HOURS

JANE ROLLED INTO the R & K Truck Stop at just past eleven in the morning. Covered in so much blood, her jeans looked black and her once white tank top looked like red tie-dye. She'd lost the hoodie somewhere along a back road. Making her way into the women's bathroom and showers, she rushed into one of the stalls and immediately stripped. She had one change of clothes in her bag—dirty clothes that smelled of Kelly Casey.

Surprisingly calm, she showered, washing the blood from her legs and body. Then washing her hair with a bottle of shampoo someone left behind, she dried off and dressed, leaving her hair wet. Before leaving the ladies' room, she shoved her bloodied clothes to the bottom of the trashcan.

She stopped in the attached convenience

store to buy a hat. Picking a knit cap from a stack in a bin, she eyed a corndog rolling on the grill.

"Anything else?" the cashier asked, looking her up and down like she was trash.

Jane shook her head, paid for her beanie and walked out the front door. Pulling the knit hat over her wet head, she walked to the side of the building where she'd left the stolen Harley. Sticking the keys in the ignition, she walked away, heading toward the bank of eighteen wheelers parked in a row beside the gas station.

The first trucker was overweight and looked like a pedophile. Jane moved along. The next one was younger—too young. Jane was afraid he might want something in return for his ride. She continued. Last on the row was a middle aged man. He walked with a limp and wore a baseball cap with an embroidered rifle that read, *I don't call 911.*

"Hey," Jane said.

"Well hello there," he replied. "Can I help you?"

"I was wondering which way you were heading out of D.C.?"

He took off his cap and scratched his head,

placing it back exactly where it had been as if he'd done it a million times. Jane suspected he had. "No place exciting. You look like you might be wanting a ride to California or something and I'm just going to boring old Cleveland."

Jane's eyes lit up. "Cleveland?"

He nodded.

"Do you mind if I tag along as far as Pittsburgh?"

"Pittsburgh? I'll have you there by suppertime. Climb in."

Jane hitched up her leg, climbing into the rig, shutting the door behind her.

"I'm Russell," he said, extending his hand.

"I'm…" Jane hesitated.

"Did you forget your name?"

Jane shook her head.

"It's okay. You don't have to tell me. That's the thing about the road, darlin'. It doesn't care who you are, just where you're going. And you seem to know where you're going."

Jane nodded. "I do."

Russell fired up the engine on the big rig. Jane placed her backpack between her feet. They pulled onto I-76 and Jane lowered her window and took a deep breath. Then digging into her backpack, she opened her tin box, thought of her friend Jennifer Drenkowski and took out one item. Turning to Russell she asked, "Do you mind if I smoke?"

DAY FOUR | 1145 HOURS

"**Y**OU WANNA TELL me what really happened?"

Charlie Madewell stared Kelly down outside the warehouse where dozens of cops, federal agents and Secret Service had descended to investigate.

"It's just like I told them. I shot Siad's counterpart after Matt Matthews shot Siad. His father just keeled over from a heart attack at the horror of the whole thing. But I have to tell you, young Matthews was there to take down Siad. His father and Siad had been working together."

Charlie gave Kelly a heavy dose of side-eye and walked away. Kelly had just made his way to his own car when he was approached again.

"Thank you for what you did."

Kelly turned and stared at the older man.

"I'm sorry. Who are you?"

Holding out an envelope he nodded to it. "Matthew wanted her to have this. I think you're the only one who will ever know how to find her again. I'm trusting you to see this home, Sergeant Casey."

"How do you know my name?"

"I'm Dr. Peter Hudson—with Maxtronix."

Kelly raised his brow in suspicion. "I see."

"I think we might be able to do some great things together, Sergeant Casey."

"Who's *we?*" Kelly asked, opening the door to his car, placing the envelope on the seat.

"You. Me. *Her.*" Peter was quiet and deliberate in his response.

Kelly nodded and looked Dr. Hudson over from head to toe.

"I don't expect you to trust me, Sergeant Casey. Not yet anyway. But someday, you might need something from me. When you do, I want you to know my door is open to you."

Peter offered his hand and Kelly shook it.

"I'm sorry for your loss today, Dr. Hudson. I think Matt was a good guy. I'm not so sure about his father."

"I'm not at liberty to discuss company

business as I'm sure you're aware—at least not at this time. I will say this, you have excellent instincts, Sergeant."

"Call me Kelly."

"Peter," he said handing Kelly a business card. "Feel free to call me. That is, when you're ready. And tell her to do the same."

Kelly nodded, but didn't say another word. Peter backed away and stepped into a limousine.

"Nice to meet you, Peter," Kelly whispered under his breath.

INSIDE THE LIMO, Peter dropped his head into his hands.

"It was going to unfold like this whether you wanted it to or not," Matteo said, his voice deep and calming. "I did everything Collie asked me to do, Peter. I warned him over and over—I even showed my face. We tried to get him to leave town."

Peter nodded, staring straight ahead. "It all feels so *wrong*."

"Collie knew there was no good way for it

to end," Matteo said. "Why do you think he sent me so many times? The man worried himself into a heart attack. I gave Matt a way out. I tried to give her a way out too. We did everything we could to help them both. Now it's over."

Peter nodded.

"What is the other envelope?" Matteo asked.

"It's a P.O. Box. I suspect it's to a reporter friend of Matt's. He wanted to make sure his name was cleared."

"Are you going to send it?"

Peter stared at the manila envelope and shook his head. "It would do more harm than good at this point."

"And what if the reporter comes around? What if this comes back to bite you in the ass?"

"I guess I'll deal with that if and when it happens."

Matteo nodded.

"Do you think we'll ever see Sergeant Casey again?"

Matteo closed his eyes and gave Peter a small shrug. "Hard to know. I'll say this, if she comes around, so will he."

"We can only hope."

"Let's get out of here, Peter. You have work to do. I need to get back to the West Wing."

DAY FIVE | 1600 HOURS

J ANE FINGERED THE studs of the leather chair as she sat on her hands in his office. The room was dark, but cozy and smelled the way she always remembered it—cigars and incense. He'd aged since the last time they'd sat together in the same room, but who was she kidding? She looked different too. He'd not even recognized her when she came down the long aisle of the church to find him at the back following the morning Mass. He confessed as he walked her to the parish offices, he thought she was a junkie coming in off the street. Jane laughed. She could think of much worse things to be thought of.

Looking like something the cat had dragged in, Father Doheny put her to bed on the couch in his office, covering her up. When she awoke, she found him quietly working behind his desk.

It was the way she always thought of him—working, praying, taking care of others.

She'd brushed her teeth in his bathroom and pulled her blonde mess of hair high on top of her head in a sloppy bun. With no clothes to change into, she'd washed a spot off the tank top she had and Father had graciously found her a fleece-lined jacket in the winter coats they'd collected for the homeless.

Now, sitting in his office, it was time. Time to gather everything he'd been keeping safe for her all these years. Now that the day had finally come, she was anxious.

At first he stared at her and Jane found her eyes begin to well with emotion. She'd learned so much about herself, her past, her family in the last twenty-four hours, she hadn't had a chance to process any of it. In true Jane fashion, she'd boxed it all up and put it on a shelf in her imaginary closet, waiting for the time and place she chose to take it all down for inspection and reflection. Father Doheny had a different idea. Dragging details out of her, she'd told him of her love for Matt—her dreams and her wishes. How conflicted she was. How she'd almost ended his life. She told him of Kelly.

How he made her feel. How his mother and father had cared for her—how it somehow made sense, but didn't.

"And how did it all end?"

Jane swallowed hard. "It ended…"

Father Doheny sat quietly, patiently. He waited for her answer. Jane wrestled with her actions. Did she tell Father what she'd done? Who she'd killed?

"It ended at the beginning."

He nodded. "Life comes full circle. And do you have anything you'd like to confess?"

Jane looked to the ceiling, the ancient chandelier flickering with an extra-bright bulb ready to blow—Jane felt the same way. Brightest and most brilliant at the very end, she felt herself fading—ready to burn out in a flash. She ran Father Doheny's question through her head. She'd ended the life of ten terrorists—ten kill assignments. She'd saved the lives of thousands. She knew she'd disrupted or even destroyed the lives of countless others that lay in the wake of her path. Matt Matthews was dead. Kelly Casey left behind. Still her ultimate goal had been accomplished. Three was dead. The Mastermind. The Instructor. The recruiter and twister of young minds. Satan on earth himself, he was the murderer of her mother and the man who'd wanted her to die in a dumpster—*her father.*

Bringing her gaze down to her hands, she realized she still had blood buried deep beneath her fingernails. "Do I have anything I want to confess?" She repeated the words with contempt for herself. "Father, I literally have blood *on* my hands."

"Tell me what you wish to confess."

With stoic reflection, Jane spoke. "I've killed people. Lots of people. I've done it because I wanted to save others—at least that's what I told myself. In the end, I think I did it for myself."

"The path of the righteous man is beset on all sides by the inequities of the selfish and the tyranny of evil men. Blessed is he, who in the name of charity and good will, shepherds the weak through the valley of darkness, for he is truly his brother's keeper and the finder of lost children."

Jane said nothing. There was nothing to be said.

"Where will you go?" he asked, pushing

toward Jane all the paperwork, passports and money associated with her new life—her new identity.

Jane shook her head. "I don't know. It's best I don't tell you."

"What will you do?"

Jane took a deep, cleansing breath. "Have a life?"

Father Doheny walked around his desk and Jane met him with a hug. "Whatever it is," he said. "Make it a good one. You've had enough pain for a few lifetimes. It's time for joy."

Pulling away, Jane nodded. "Father, I have just one favor to ask."

"Anything."

"Will you mail something for me?"

DAY FIVE | 1800 HOURS

J ANE SAT IN the booth at the local diner waiting for her dinner to arrive. She had decisions to make and for once she wasn't doing it on an empty stomach. When the blue plate special arrived, she sat back and smiled. Meatloaf and mashed potatoes with gravy and a side of green beans. Taking the photo of her mother out of her backpack, she sat it beside her. In her own little world, she fantasized this was the kind of meal her mom would've made her growing up.

The television blared over the diner bar as the national nightly news began to air.

"Terrorists taken down in Washington D.C. We'll speak with America's hero tonight, Sergeant Kelly Casey of the NYPD Hercules Team. How can America protect itself from the impending threat of ISIS?"

Jane smiled and let out a snort and ordered a Coke. When Kelly Casey's face appeared on the screen, she dropped her fork and listened intently.

"I can't take credit for this. Matt Matthews of Maxtronix, who unfortunately lost his life in this horrible raid was the mastermind and the hero."

"Yes, Sergeant Casey," the reporter interjected. "We're learning as this unfolds, Matt Matthews, heir to the billion dollar weapons manufacturer, had been working undercover for the government."

Jane watched as Kelly looked directly into the camera. "As I said, *he* is the real hero. He and nameless others who do their job to keep our citizens safe every day, right under the noses of the American people." Kelly looked away from the reporter and into the camera. "And you know who you are."

Jane turned from the screen and smiled, taking a drink of the Coke the waitress set in front of her. "How's the meatloaf, honey?"

She nodded. "It's good."

Pointing to the screen. "Would you look at that? Those hero types are always so freakin' hot. You know?"

Jane looked at Kelly Casey on the screen. The stern and determined look in his eyes *was* sexy. "Yeah," she said. "I know."

"Up next, reports of unexplained explosions all across Pakistan and Iraq. Is ISIS testing weapons? Or are the extremists playing with fire trying to reverse engineer American war machines? We'll speak with retired General Richard Painswick."

Jane shook her head at the sight of her former commanding officer. He was older, but still looked as ornery as ever. Just as the news went to a break, General *Bring the Pain* gave a soundbite. "Hell, if they wanna blow themselves up, I can guaran-damn-tee you we aren't going to do anything to stop them."

DAY FIVE | 1900 HOURS

THE SUN SET over the horizon and a chill came upon Jane quickly. She zipped up the front of the fleece lined jacket Father Doheny had given her. She needed to buy something new. She had thousands in cash and a new credit card, driver's license and passport burning a hole in her backpack. The world was hers for the taking. She just needed to take it.

Holding two red roses in her hands, she laid them on the grave and stood back. She'd never been to a cemetery before—at least not to see anyone. She didn't know what to say, or if she was supposed to say anything at all.

"Thank you."

They were the only words that seemed fitting.

Taking a seat on the cold grass, she decided to just *be* for a moment. The cemetery was quiet and as the sun went down, she found it a proper way to say goodbye.

Staring at the headstone, she lost herself. So much so, she didn't hear his car pull up or his door shut.

"I thought I might find you here."

Jane didn't stand, but turned and squinted into the western sun, looking directly up at Kelly Casey. "Are you here to arrest me?"

He sat down beside her, cross-legged at the foot of his parents' grave. "And lose my status as the best terrorist slayer ever? No way."

They both stared at the pink sky over Jacob and Elizabeth Casey's headstone but said nothing. Kelly put his arm around Jane and kissed her on the temple. "Are you okay?"

She nodded.

Reaching into his coat pocket, he pulled out an envelope with only one word on the top—*Jane*.

"Peter Hudson gave this to me. Matt left it for you. I think he knew what was going to happen."

Jane looked at the envelope long and hard before she took it from Kelly's hands.

She opened it to find a USB drive and a

handwritten letter.

Kelly stood and walked away, giving her space. Jane read.

Dear Jane,

I've whispered your name alone in the dark for days on end. It was the wrong name, but it was you all the same. I think I've been whispering your name all my life, not knowing who you would be, but waiting for you to arrive. You, with your disarming blue eyes. You, with your tank tops and jeans and the horrible backpack you refuse to be without. You with your perfect bottom I could pick out anywhere, anytime. You, with your good heart and sound judgement. You had every chance to do what you were asked and didn't. For that, I thank you. It gave me the opportunity to do what I wanted most, clear my name and rid the world of a man who'd turned my personal life upside down. He tried to take the rest of us with him. I couldn't allow it to happen.

If this letter has found its way to you, then as I suspected, ending the life of The Instructor did not go well enough for me to tell you how I feel about you in person.

Now that I'm gone there are a few things I want you to remember—about me—about us. You're strong, brave and beautiful and although the time we shared was short, I didn't need forever to know that I loved you. I knew it the moment I met you in the library. Now that I won't be around to fight for you, just know that whomever the lucky man to have you until your dying day might be, even if he loved you with all the power of his soul for a whole lifetime, he couldn't love you as much as I did in a single day. I'll take the time we shared to my grave and I can promise you I'll be waiting to see your perfect ass on the other side.

Finally, everything you need to know is on this USB drive. I'm leaving it all in your capable hands. There's nothing to do, just accounting to understand. And if you have any questions or need help, Dr. Peter Hudson is a good man. You can trust him.

Now, don't be alarmed when you see the amount attached to this. It's big. Remember, Jane, it's just numbers and it's only money— blood money. Now clean and untraceable, do something good with it. Use it to fight the good fight. I know you will.

Until we meet again my love, I'll be with you always,
Matt.

Jane folded the note back and slipped it into the envelope, placing the USB drive into her pocket.

"You okay?" Kelly asked.

Jane stood to meet him, but said nothing. She was numb. Numb with emotion, numb with knowledge, numb to everything. If she tried to pack one more feeling into her heart and head she would self-destruct.

"Hey." Kelly turned her around and pulled her close. "I'm not going anywhere and you're not getting rid of me. I'm not allowing you to peel me off of you while you move on. We've got something here. I know you feel it."

Jane looked him in the eyes. The kind eyes that had taken her in, explained her life to her in a way she'd never known. It was true, she did feel a connection to him, but based on past history, Jane believed that she only brought misery and pain to those who dared to care for her.

"Look," Kelly said, taking her hands into

his. "I was the key to your past, but…" He hesitated and Jane looked away only to have him lift her chin with his finger. "What I'm saying is, what if you're the key to my future? *Our* future? Don't you believe in divine intervention? Even just a little bit?"

"I don't know what I believe in anymore, Kelly."

"Do you believe in me?"

Jane bit her lip and looked beyond Kelly into the fleeting light of day as if it would provide an answer.

"It's not a hard question, Jane. Do you believe in me?"

Jane brought her gaze back to him and answered honestly. "Yes, I believe in you."

A slow grin painted across Kelly's face. "That's all I needed to hear because I believe in you, Jane. I believe in *us*."

Jane dropped Kelly's hands and walked away.

"Hey," he called after her. "Where are you going?"

Jane stopped and turned. Jane looked back.

"I have no idea. You wanna come?"

DAY SIX | 1203 HOURS

J ACK BLUE WAS late for work. His baby girl sick with an ear infection, he and his girlfriend had been up all night. Now trading off during the day to stay with her, they'd both begged time off from work to take her to the free clinic. Money was too tight for a doctor or a baby sitter and yet they were both on the verge of losing their hourly jobs to even get her the care she needed, let alone the antibiotics which were more than their grocery budget for the week.

"Blue!" his manager called out to him with a look of unforgiving disgust. "I said you could be a little late, not an hour late."

"I'm sorry, dude. The clinic was packed and we had to wait our turn. I had to get my old lady and the baby back to the apartment and we had to stop at the drugstore—"

"Look at my face, Blue. Do I look like I care? I've had to move everyone's lunch break because you couldn't make it in when you said."

Jack tossed his scarred hands in the air. "I'm sorry. That's all I can say."

"This is your last warning. If you're late again, you're fired. Got it?"

Jack nodded. "I got it."

"By the way," his manger said, sliding a manila envelope across the checkout counter. "Stop using the business as your personal address."

"Wha?"

The manager shook his head at Jack, watching him look over the envelope. "Just get to work. Okay?"

Out of sight, Jack opened the large envelope. Inside was a handwritten letter attached by paperclip to another white business envelope.

Dear Jack—

Thank you for your help. Sorry I won't be able to meet your girlfriend or daughter. People like us can't do much for one another except be there. It's something you once told me. This is me being there for you. Follow your passion for art. I know you'll make many people happy if you'll only share your gift. You always managed to make me happy.

J.D.

p.s. Do me a favor and don't draw dicks.

Puzzled, Jack opened the envelope and found a Cashier's Check made out to him, Jackson Blue, for five hundred thousand dollars.

With a gasp, Jack grabbed his chest.

"What are you standing around for, Blue? Get your ass to work."

Jack's stare morphed into a sneer. "I'm going home to my sick baby."

"Then you're fired."

"You can't fire me, asshole. I quit."

DAY FIFTEEN | 0500 HOURS

Somewhere in Syria…

THE CAVE WAS dark and well lived in. Like bats, they'd hung around long enough to stay under the radar, but soon they'd need to relocate again. Theirs was a traveling band and darkness was their greatest ally.

"Sir," one said, reporting to the ranking superior of the clan. "Word is we are losing drones all over."

A single wrinkle pinched between his young, blue eyes. "How?"

The messenger shook his head. "We don't know. They believe they are self-destructing."

The young man paused before continuing. "And?"

"There's more, sir."

Dressed in traditional garments of a thawb and bisht, his rank was easy to spot and he gave his undivided attention to the messenger. "What is it?"

"I bring news of your father, the great Siad al Daleel ul Khyayraat."

"Yes?"

"He is dead. Killed in America."

The young man showed no emotion as he stared into the darkness of the cave. "His bloodshed shall be a curse that will chase the Americans and their agents. A curse that will pursue them inside and out. We will continue to plan and plot without fatigue, boredom, despair, surrender or indifference. They will neither enjoy nor live in security."

"Sir, our allegiance is now to you. What do you want to do?"

"Bring his killer to me."

———————————

Kris Calvert is a former copywriter and PR mercenary who after some coaxing, began writing novels. She loves alliteration, pearls and post-it notes. She's married to the man of her dreams and lives in Lexington, Kentucky. She's Momma to two grown children and is also responsible for one very needy dog. When she's not writing, she's baking cupcakes.

WEBSITE: www.kriscalvert.com

EMAIL: info@kriscalvert.com

TWITTER: @kriscalvert

FACEBOOK:
www.facebook.com/kriscalvert30

BLOG: www.calvertwrites.blogspot.com

NEWSLETTER
www.kriscalvert.com/Kris_Calvert/NEWSLE
TTER.html

www.ingramcontent.com/pod-product-compliance
Lightning Source LLC
Chambersburg PA
CBHW051638180726
48284CB00006B/1783